About the authors

Since *A Melon for Ecstasy* was published in 1971 John Fortune has acted on television and in the theatre and written scripts for television and film. In the early nineties Rory Bremner invited him to join John Bird in writing for his show. This led to the adlibbed conversations with John Bird which won them the British Comedy Award for Top Male Performers in 1995 and the Bafta Award for Best Light Entertainment Performance in 1996.

John Wells was born in 1936. He read Modern Languages at Oxford, before going on to teach at Eton. While teaching he also wrote satirical sketches and made appearances at a nightclub in Soho, leading to the scandalous newspaper headline, 'Eton master peddles smut'. He left his teaching job to become a full-time satirist and was a founder member of *Private Eye*, for which he and Richard Ingrams wrote *Mrs Wilson's Diary* and the *Dear Bill* letters. From then on he combined work as an actor, humorist and comic impressionist, as a columnist, script writer and translator of plays and operas and as a playwright and director. He died in 1998.

PRION HUMOUR CLASSICS

Augustus Carp, Esq	Henry Howarth Bashford
Seven Men and Two Others	Max Beerbohm
How to Travel Incognito	Ludwig Bemelmans
The Freaks of Mayfair	E F Benson
Mapp and Lucia	E F Benson
The Marsh Marlowe Letters	Craig Brown
How Steeple Sinderby Wanderers Won the FA Cup	J L. Carr
The Diary of a Provincial Lady*	E M Delafield
The Papers of A J Wentworth, BA	H F Ellis
Squire Haggard's Journal	Michael Green
The Diary of a Nobody	George and Weedon Grossmith
Three Men in a Boat	Jerome K Jerome
Mrs Caudle's Curtain Lectures	Douglas Jerrold
The Unspeakable Skipton	Pamela Hansford Johnson
Sunshine Sketches of a Little Town	Stephen Leacock
No Mother to Guide Her	Anita Loos
Here's Luck	Lennie Lower
The Autobiography of a Cad	A G Macdonell
The Serial*	Cyra McFadden
The World of S J Perelman*	S J Perelman
The Education of Hyman Kaplan*	Leo Rosten
The Return of Hyman Kaplan*	Leo Rosten
The Unrest-Cure and Other Beastly Tales	Saki
The English Gentleman	Douglas Sutherland
My Life and Hard Times*	James Thurber
A Touch of Daniel	Peter Tinniswood
Cannibalism in the Cars	Mark Twain

*For copyright reasons these titles are not available in the USA or Canada in the Prion edition.

A Melon for Ecstasy

JOHN FORTUNE &
JOHN WELLS

with a new introduction by
JOHN FORTUNE

PRION

This edition published 2002 by
Prion Books Limited
Imperial Works, Perren Street,
London NW5 3ED
www.prionbooks.com

First published in 1971
Copyright © 1971 John Fortune and John Wells
Introduction © 2002 John Fortune

ISBN 1-85375-470-6

Jacket design by Keenan
Jacket image Panoptika
Printed and bound in Great Britain by
Creative Print & Design Ltd., Ebbw Vale

'A Woman for duty,
A Boy for pleasure,
But a Melon for ecstasy.'
            Old Turkish Proverb

INTRODUCTION
by JOHN FORTUNE

I am sitting with John Wells in the back of a black taxi one spring day in the late sixties. We are on our way, I suppose, from John's studio in Scarsdale Villas to the Television Centre at White City. Waiting at the lights by the Cromwell Road John tells me a story. K, a young man of our acquaintance left university and joined the all-powerful News and Current Affairs Department of BBC Television. Last Monday, through a combination of illness and other more senior producers making films all over the world, he finds himself, in his early thirties, in charge of the whole department. Forty or so producers and journalists cram into his office to be given their orders for the week. One of the producers makes a little speech congratulating K on his sudden elevation. As he is doing so K's pretty young secretary bursts into the room shouting 'YOU NEVER TOLD ME YOU WERE MARRIED!!!'

The traffic lights changed to green. The lights had been turning green all through the sixties. Sex, we thought, was an island our parents had scarcely mapped. We were wrong of course, but that only added to our determination. John quoted to me the Turkish proverb: 'A woman for duty, a boy for pleasure, but a melon for ecstasy'.

But why stop at melons? Making love to trees might bring out the Wordsworth in all of us.

At the time I was living in Scotland, renting a romantic castle at the foot of Glen Shee for twelve pounds a week. In the paddock at the front of the house was an enormous Sequoia tree. It was fashionable to plant these in the 1820s, because, as some local laird explained to me, the reddish bark, inches thick and very soft, made the trunk a perfect punch bag for bare-knuckle boxers to practise on. The idea of growing a tree a hundred and fifty feet tall for such a purpose seemed on the face of it extravagant, but perhaps there were other, less obvious uses to which this giant member of the bald cypress family (*Taxodiaceae*) might be put.

John came up to Perthshire and we wrote the book in three weeks. It was a perfect place to work. Outside the house were a thousand acres of possible lovers in full leaf. Inside, the castle offered daily comic possibilities. Writing in the library one morning we were interrupted by our cleaning lady Mrs Sinclair, looking pale and shaken, who explained that she had banged her head on a stone lintel. We sat her down and gave her whisky. Next morning, coming back to the library from making coffee, John noticed Mrs Sinclair down the corridor banging her head against the wall.

John would write the book in longhand while I stood on the carpet in front of the fire practising my putting stroke and remembering my golf teacher's summation of my gifts: 'John, to save your life, you couldn't hit a cow's arse with a banjo'.

But despite the distractions the manuscript pile grew. I have never known anyone who enjoyed a joke more than

John. It wasn't something that just happened in his head. He ingested the joke and it modified his whole body. I was reminded of John one day wading about in a warm, shallow sea and seeing cuttle fish sending nerve signals down their bodies which turned into neon displays of iridescent colour. Not that John resembled anything fishy. His was a foxy look. It might have been knowing that his father was a vicar in the Church of England that put you in mind of a naughty priest, though more monseigneur than Anglican. Naughtiness in the Church of England leans towards the gay, because, I suppose, their priests are licenced to be heterosexual. John would have made the perfect leading man for Carry On Cardinal. He loved gossip, and hearing confession is like hearing gossip, the sexier the better, but without the boredom of having to keep it secret.

Of course, in Britain gossip becomes more interesting the higher up the class system it occurs. John was drawn to the upper classes like Degas to dancers. It was mainly because their need to reproduce themselves led them to more and more comic sexual manoeuvres. We shared the opinion that aristocrats had evolved small feet the better to creep around the corridors of stately homes. I told him about a friend up the glen who found himself next to a beautiful girl at a country-house dinner. After flirting with her through the meal he was thrilled to be invited to come to her bedroom at two in the morning. He spent two hours of delicious anticipation in his room, bathing and scenting himself, polishing his teeth, wrapping himself in a silk dressing gown and then at two o'clock precisely, tip-toed to the girl's door, tapped softly and opened it. 'Hello, Rhoddy,' she whispered, 'don't turn on the light. I'm over here.' Rhoddy took off his dressing gown, made his way to her bed and climbed in. Whereupon the girl turned on her bedside light to reveal a large man lying next to her, saying 'I think you've met my husband Arthur, haven't you?'

Soon after we finished the book we collaborated on a television programme in a series called 'One Pair of Eyes'. In the film John visits me in Perthshire and we discuss aspects of death in a mock academic way while in the background people from the porter carrying John's luggage at the station to the camera man shooting the film succumb to the reaper. We walk through a herd of cattle discussing Goethe's view of death in nature and fail to notice one of the cows keel over. It's strange to think that while the prop man was jerking the nylon line to topple the stuffed cow the seeds of John's death were floating around his bloodstream. As, I suppose they were in the prop man and you and me. And had been in the stuffed cow. John came up with the title for the film: 'Step Laughing Into the Grave' and the BBC transmitted it the following Easter.

Which reminds me of a couplet of Dryden which John was fond of. I doubt if I remember it accurately but it was along the lines of:

And well God knows how little mirth
Will keep the Soul of man on earth.

He is missed.

Chiswick. October 2001.

Foreword

The months described in these pages – 'leaves' being a word too charged with meaning for me to be used in so neutral a context – were among the most dramatic of my life, forming as they did both a lens through which my self was rendered visible to me in microscopic detail, and a crucible in which the impurities of my spirit were burned out.

It is not shame that has delayed the publication of this record – rather do I glory in my ordeal, hoping that it may serve as an inspiration to other lovers of Nature – but only the difficulty, after so many autumns, of gathering from yellowed archives in the confusion of bureau drawers the fragments of coloured glass that compose this kaleidoscope. Shall I shake it? Gentle reader, the toy is in your hands.

H.M.
Slippery Elms,
New Forest.
19–

Part One

EXCERPT FROM THE DIARY OF HUMPHREY MACKEVOY

I am just back from the garden. The moonlight is bright enough to write by, and casts the shadow of my tree – sleeper's head across a pillow - over the page. My thighs are still cold from the bark, and that instrument of my pleasure is tenderly vibrating, wet with our ecstasy. We did well tonight, my proud battering ram! Singing like a nightingale in the dark wood, filling up the night with sweetness.

And the tree! My Tree of Heaven! *Ailanthus alttssinia!* Nat pointed it out to me as we came back from our walk just before tea. 'It's Japanese,' he said, and I knew I had to have it. I looked up into the bare branches as we went into the conservatory, my eyelids already heavy with secret lust. The immense bifurcations, the endlessly spreading limbs! All through tea I watched it, causing Bee to pour hot water over my wrist as I held out my cup for more.

I must try to set down, while the memory is still with me, how this act of love was different. There was something about the texture of the bark under my exploring fingers, the density of the torn white wood, above all the temperature against that most sensitive part of my body. Immediately I entered, clumsily tearing aside my dressing gown to feel the…*

* Here the manuscript breaks off. H.M.

3

Mummy can't move the toes of her left foot. She called me just then to tell me. She thinks it's spreading up her legs. I reassured her, collected the bedclothes, and put them back on the bed. I hope she didn't wake Nat and Bee. I'm so sleepy. The moon has risen above the Tree of Heaven and is smaller and colder. I can't remember anything specific about it now; was it the scent of the bark? The shadowy cleft of the bole? The delicate tracery above me? No…you *were* inscrutable!

Minx! Jade! There is a temple bell inside you that I *rang*. Goodnight.

FROM THE MUNDHAM POLICE STATION BEAT INFORMATION BOOK

In accordance with Insp. Stoneley's instructions to keep an eye open for the borings I carefully scrutinized the plane trees in Kimberley Drive. Two had been defaced by the Borer, one showing signs of recent activity.

(Signed) R. Makins 76 Constable.

CUTTING FROM THE *Mundham Advertiser*

Holes Mystery

Drillings Continue

Puzzlement is the keynote at the Mayoral Chambers this week as baffling holes continue to appear among our trees. The latest victims would appear to be the plane trees in Kimberley Drive, sometime home of the late Mr Alfred Widgett, donator of the Memorial Bench and Dog Fountain.

Large Bird

One theory advanced by the Town Clerk, Mr Chas Smart, is that the damage has been inflicted by a species of large bird, incensed perhaps by the lopping, on the part of the Council, of the trees' upper branches. 'The reason for the lopping,' Mr Smart told the Advertiser, 'was the unsightly appearance of the branches. Steps are however being taken to bring the menace under control.'

EXCERPT FROM THE MINUTES OF THE MUNDHAM
ORNITHOLOGICAL SOCIETY

Referring to the recent devastations in the area, the President, Miss Ethne Longridge OM, DSO and Bar, said that in her opinion the culprit was in all probability the rare Fringed Woodpecker, last seen in these islands at the end of the last century by the President herself. The perforations, she said, had all been made at a height of thirty-three inches above the ground, and this in itself was an exciting discovery. Her secretary, Miss Longridge continued, had further discovered that all of these borings were at an angle of between fifteen and twenty degrees to the horizontal, a fact previously noted in Farjeon's monograph on the habits of the Woodpecker, 'Hoorah for the Wye Valley!' Her theory, Miss Longridge said, was that the little visitor, a migrant from Scandinavia, was forced in his native habitat to make his holes just above the snow line, which Miss Longridge could avow, on the basis of a holiday spent in Norway in the summer of 1932, was usually about three feet or slightly less. A resolution was passed unanimously that a telegram be sent to the Royal Ornithological Society stating the findings, and another to the Town Clerk's Office, threatening a High Court Injunction should any attempt be made to trap, snare, net or gin the rare visitor.

POSTCARD, 5 $\frac{1}{2}$″ X 3 $\frac{1}{2}$″, WITH AN EARLY PHOTOGRAPH ON THE OBVERSE, FROM HUMPHREY MACKEVOY TO MRS BEATRICE GROSS

My dear Mrs Gross,

Mother and I did so enjoy the weekend at Bars. Mother has hardly stopped talking about it ever since. She was much better after we got home, and Dr Burton said he thought the stroke must have been a false alarm. Dr Phillips isn't so sure, but we must all be very calm. Mother is lying down at the moment, but sends her love. She wonders whether by any chance she left a blue bottle behind with some brown and yellow pills inside? I think they would have been in the cabinet in our bathroom. Mother says not to put yourself out, but should anyone be coming in to Mundham she would be eternally grateful. Hope you like the PC. One of a batch that came into the shop the other day. I think the couple are charming. How lovely it must have been to live in those days! Running out of space so must close. Thank you again. Yours sincerely, H. Mackevoy.

P.S. Mummy says she's sending the travelling rug back by parcel post as soon as it's been cleaned.

LETTER TO THE *Mundham Advertiser* FROM MRS POLLOCK

> Sir, I was horrified to learn of Mr Smart's plan ('It's War on Feathered Fiends says Smart'*) to paint all the trees in the Alderman Thornton Park

* I have been unable to trace this cutting, though the wording of the statement is typical of the man. H.M.

and Recreation Centre with bird repellent. Is there not enough suffering in the world without this? If, as has been suggested (where was Mr Smart in the War?) the bird responsible for the tree damage is a rare visitor to these shores, to wit the Fringed Woodpecker, should not might and main be exercised in its defence? On the most mercenary level it could become the type of tourist attraction our community so badly needs. And how would Mr Smart like it, when visiting foreign parts, were he to find himself repelled by noxious chemicals? Mr Smart would be better employed doing something about the filthy bus shelters and Negroes in our fair community.

I am, Sir, Yours Truly,

F. C. Pollock (Mrs)
14, Hooper Drive,
Ringwood Estate.

LETTER TO INSPECTOR STONELEY FROM MRS BEATRICE GROSS

Dear Inspector Stoneley,

I *do* hope you won't mind my writing to you personally, but you were so *marvellous* about Nat's trouble last year. Something has happened about which I would *adore* to have your advice.

As you may know, our friend Mr Smart has been trying to discourage these woodpecker things with his beastly sprays. With the result, *now*, that they seem to have come over to us. I can't allow my husband out with his gun, as you know, and I suppose we'd have Miss Longridge down on us like a ton of bricks even if I could. I do hate the idea of DDT and things. I was wondering whether a constable couldn't be spared to rally round.

Could you be *really* adorable, do you think, and take the thing in hand?

Yours ever,

Beatrice Gross.

LETTER TO THE *Mundham Advertiser* FROM ARCHDEACON HORNS

Dear Sir,
May I enter the lists on behalf of the Fringed Woodpecker, *Gecinus Fimbreatus?* This has been, I am convinced, a case of mistaken identity. I myself have seen the culprit at work on several occasions red-handed. The animal, rather than bird, in question is a species of the sabre-toothed dormouse, hitherto known to us only from fossils as *Myoxus Horribilis*, a freak survival of the plasticene age. The little animal, whose teeth outweigh its body in a ratio of eighty to one, needed, or I should say, needs, an enormous quantity of larvae to maintain its calcium balance, and indeed to maintain its balance at all. This, then, is the creature which I have seen. Small, hunched, with a russet fur coat, amazingly dentate, furtive and

moving rather like a pole-vaulter towards its burrow not far from the Corporation Rubbish Tip. Surely a few ravaged trees are a small price to pay for having in our midst one of God's first experiments in the dormouse field?

Yours etc,

T. Horns (Archdeacon Rtd),
Merrilees Hospital,
Mundham.

EXCERPT FROM THE DIARY OF HUMPHREY MACKEVOY

I must have passed it a thousand times without noticing it. Just one of a long row in Kimberley Drive. How could I have been so blind? And then after a miserable day at the shop, last night, just as it was getting dark... How shall I explain it? A little leaf came drifting down and settled on the shoulder of my overcoat. I looked up, hardly able to grasp the innocence of that gentle overture. The maimed shoulders, the slender trunk. I felt my loins stir. But then, overcome with nervousness, I walked on.

Mummy noticed something was wrong when I got home. I skipped tea, and went straight to the shed to begin that sweet oiling of the drill that is the delicious prelude to a night of bliss. Unveiling the brace and bit is a moment I dwell on in my dreams with a special ecstasy. It's such a marvellous piece of work. The balance, the smooth clicking of the ratchet, the firm mahogany grip, chestnut–dark – all the chestnuts I've known have been dark – it seems so harmless, swinging there in my hand. And yet...

I hurried out, my feet swishing through the fallen leaves, breathing the edge of frost and woodsmoke in the air. It was turned away from me, my tall lovely, looking towards the tennis courts. Branches raw-cut, its trunk unprotected. A moment later the steel bit touched the pale bark. I threw my whole weight against it, turning like a madman. The bright steel, furrowed and sharpened, disappeared spinning to the shank, casting back moist white curls of virgin wood. I span the drill again in the opposite direction, withdrawing the glinting head, its threads choked with pulp. Then, oh God, the rest followed swiftly. I was naked under my Crombie overcoat. The bark was wet and cold against my flanks, my fingernails sank deep into the lichen as I thrust myself savagely into the passage tunnelled by the churning drill.

Later, much later, clinging to its strong uprightness like a drowning man, feeling its sap and mine oozing down the bole and dripping from my trembling knees, I heard footsteps approaching from the direction of Strawberry Lane. Quickly retrieving my brace and bit and buttoning my overcoat I hurried home, aching with giddy triumphs, and slipped into a soft erotic slumber.

It was only this morning, as I was examining myself for splinters, that I became aware of a dull burning sensation. Some of my pubic hair had been bleached. Much of the rest was singed, and as I combed it a good deal fell out, brittle and carbonized. The membrane itself is unharmed, though the sense of burning irritation continues. I have never touched an infected tree before, though I have often dreaded it. My heart hammers wildly as I consider what might happen. To be out of action for weeks on end, to be forced to submit to the clumsy proddings of Dr Phillips… I did what I could with the Germolene and an old fingerstall I found in the airing cupboard and hurried down to kiss Mummy.

I can never pass a tree of the night before without a choking sense of shame. The cruel daylight reveals too clearly the folly of it, our weird incompatibility. Usually I quicken my step and avert my gaze, half feeling on the back of my neck the tree's reproach. This time, however, I felt I had to grit my teeth and force myself to look more closely. I noticed that the surface of the bole had a shiny appearance, as though recently varnished. I stroked it with my finger, a gesture so different from the night before, and found that my fingertip was discoloured by a brown sulphurous substance.

Puzzled, I walked on. In the park, men in blue overalls were spraying other trees. Not daring to ask what they were about, I went to the shop, where I discovered the truth in Monday's paper. I cannot say what I would like to do to Mr Smart, but it would not be pleasant.

EXCERPT FROM THE MINUTES OF THE MUNDHAM
ORNITHOLOGICAL SOCIETY

Referring to a correspondence* she had had with the Town Clerk, Mr Chas Smart, the President, Miss Ethne Longridge, OM, DSG and Bar, said that she had received assurances to the effect that the present precautions were intended solely to protect the well-being of the trees, and that the substance in use could not cause any harm or irritation to migrants. Municipal trees only were affected, and birds would be encouraged to congregate in privately-owned trees and gardens.

Mrs Townsend, an *ex officio* member of the Sightings Committee, reported having seen what she believed to be the Fringed Woodpecker sitting on a lampshade in the corner of the Railway Arms Lounge Bar. She described its song as a recurrent deep and reverberating hiccup. It did not seem to be in the least afraid of her, and indeed asked

* This appears to be lost. H.M

11

her to render another chorus of 'Annie Laurie' which it accompanied with wild flapping of its wings and a rotary motion of the eyes. The Committee regretfully accepted Mrs Townsend's resignation, and there being no further business the meeting was adjourned.

MEMO TO MR CHAS SMART, THE TOWN CLERK FROM THE
PARKS SUPERINTENDENT, ALDERMAN STRANGEWAYS

Dear Mr Smart,

Concerning the current crash spraying programme *vis-à-vis* Borough Trees it has been brought to my notice that the present ornicide currently in use, namely Spinelli's CH_3ooH6 'Fethoblast', comes out on computation of cubic foot cost-effectiveness at no less than 3/- per square foot of tree treated. Whilst not wishing to look in the mouth Signor F. Guillonotti's generous arrangements, whereby your brother-in-law has made available stocks of War Surplus ornicides at allegedly reduced prices, I do feel it is time we all had a long cool look.

More especially in view of certain revelations that Mrs Brenda Littlejohn, of the Oatings, Albuhera Walk, is prepared to make, in public if necessary, viz. that in at least one instance the Italian Product has been found wanting by the Woodpecker. In one tree previously treated in Albuhera Walk she has noted fresh borings, and more may well come to light.

Whilst admitting that we have not always seen eye to eye on all matters in the past, I assume you will endorse my decision to introduce, for an indefinite trial period, Hooper's New Biological 'Birdoff', which I am informed is an excellent product, and used by five out of six Penguin Control Stations on the Antarctic Ice Cap. I am furthermore convinced that a saturation impact policy is the only viable means if we are to stamp out this vicious intruder into our community. The Birdoff product at the end of the day pans out at an incredible 2/7d per square foot of tree treated (less, I understand, bulk forward buying discounts), fully justifying in my view an immediate 100% increase in spray effort to include all trees, shrubs and exposed wooden surfaces both in the public and the private sector.

These modifications to be with effect from yesterday morning.

Yours faithfully,

L. Strangeways
Honorary Superintendent of Parks.

EXCERPT FROM THE DIARY OF HUMPHREY MACKEVOY

Worse today. One of the old splinter scars has turned orange. It may be the Mercurochrome, but I am not sure. I have tried everything. Yesterday I walked about with it inside a test tube full of crushed ice, strapped to my thigh with thick rubber bands. Today I have dispensed with the ice and must try to grin and bear it. The pain is intolerable. Three times this morning already a customer has sent me climbing up to the top of the ladder in search of a book about birds.

Now the shop is quiet and I can sit and eat my sandwiches. If it isn't looking up by tomorrow I'll have to mention it to Dr Phillips when he comes to see Mummy. If only the desire would leave me as the ability has! There's a little willow by the pond in the park. Just to think of it leaning to admire its reflection in the still water...The pain! I must try and put it out of my mind.

I have just acquired a nice copy of the 1743 Shenton Edition of the *Pilgrim's Progress*. Some pages a little foxed, but otherwise in good condition. Oh willow, willow, willow!

Stop it. Go and buy some stamps.

MEMO FROM THE TOWN CLERK, MR CHAS SMART TO
ALDERMAN L. STRANGEWAYS, THE PARKS SUPERINTENDENT

Sir,

It was not my intention to reply to you otherwise than
through the good offices of the Borough Engineer's
Solicitors, Messrs Gwatkin, Cazenove and Hitler, but
bearing in mind the desirability of avoiding a public scandal
and also in view of your helpful attitude towards my
daughter Pamela's spot of bother last Easter, I offer the
following advice.

No one but a lunatic would be unaware of the
exceedingly close relationship between Hooper Birdoff
Products and the Strangeways Low-Cal Domestic
Burgundy Corporation, *viz.* that the former is a recently
incorporated direct subsidiary of the latter. In the light of
this, your proposed action, under the provisions of the
Public Bodies Corrupt Practices Act of 1889, could be very
deleterious to your personal liberty. Furthermore, even
were your crude ruse less transparent, I would be most
loath to accept the evidence of Mrs Littlejohn, your sister-
in-law, involved as she was in the scandalous Doughnut
Epidemic episode at the High School in 1953.

I myself have been more than satisfied with the Spinelli
product. Disregarding Mrs Littlejohn's evidence there have
been no further borings, and the saturation drench you
propose, as Mrs Townsend of the Ornithological Society
has pointed out,* could only exacerbate the ecological
imbalance. I give you forty-eight hours to revoke your
orders, pending which time all operatives under this
Office's direct control will continue to mount Operation

* Apparently by word of mouth, as I can find no printed or written
statement of this warning. H.M.

14

Sticky with tried and trusted Fethoblast. As to your threatened incursions into the private sector, I am flabbergasted by your apparent contempt for the basic liberties of the individual. Those operatives under your control would be well advised to return to their homes and avoid trouble.

Yours faithfully,

Chas Smart.

EXCERPT FROM THE DIARY OF HUMPHREY MACKEVOY

I am almost completely bald in the left groin this morning, and my sheets look like the floor of a hairdresser's shop! What am I to do? Hell and destruction! Fortunately the colour is a little better today, and the swelling is down far enough to recognize some old features. I would like to put Mr Smart's head through a mangle. What harm have I done to them?

Dr Phillips comes this afternoon. I could catch him in the hall as he goes out, but what am I to say? That I used the same bathwater as Mummy? That I have been in a public lavatory? That I've made love to a woman? And what could he do about it that I haven't already done? Saw a long-trunked sapling today, an elm, just on the brink of treehood. Slender branches lifted and a scar on the trunk at exactly the right height. The pain! I shall go mad!

LETTER FROM MISS ETHINE LONGRIDGE, OM, DSO AND BAR TO INSPECTOR STONELEY

My dear Reggie,

What a relief to get your dear letter after all these years. I had feared that what you crossly termed my priggishness had separated me from your affections. How glad I am that

15

this is not the case. And I do hope that at some future date you will permit me to explain to you my reasons for striking you that afternoon in Humper's Dingle.

But to the business in hand. I rushed at once to my Flanegan's, and I can assure you that there is no reason to doubt the veracity of your hypothesis concerning the Woodpecker at Bars House. Staple food it is indeed! Dear man, you have the mind of a true Ornithologist. Must fly.

Affectionate greetings,

Ethne.

REPORT BY INSPECTOR STONELEY TO CID READING

At the request of Mrs B. Gross of Bars House, Mundham, I visited the aforesaid lady's garden to investigate a complaint in connection with the recent borings outbreak. In previous cases the Borings have been effected in Municipal trees, surrounded either by a hard asphalt surface or by parkland turf. In this instance however, a fine sixty-foot specimen of the Tree of Heaven or Stinking Elm variety (approximate value, I am informed, £700), the surrounding soil bore the clear imprint of a left and a right foot, suggesting considerable propinquity to the tree at the time when the offence was committed. This is a new development.

I also observed what appeared to be the outline of a brace and bit-like object some eighteen inches from the tree, the imprint suggesting that it had been thrown down from a height of about three foot six into the moist soil. Moreover experiments in my own laboratory indicate that the 138 specimens of wood shaving so far collected are consistent with such a tool having been used. I have further to report that the footprints, which appeared to be of a fully-grown, unclothed male or female of indeterminate height and weight, and dubious age, though probably brunette, approached the tree in a stealthy manner via the greenhouse (see attached map) and returned to the house by route B in what seems to have been some haste.

I was at first at a loss as to how I should equate such evidence with the Woodpecker Theory. However on reexamining the footprints it was borne in upon me that there was a suspect I had overlooked. I refer to the Malayan Orang-Outang (in the Malay tongue Orang, Man, Outang, Of The Woods). We all know that this russet-haired primate preys upon the woodpecker, its *Staple Diet*. Lucky the escaped Orang-Outang who finds in Mundham such an abundant supply of his favourite food! In a flash I recognized the size, shape, weight, stride and colouring of our intruder. How natural that he should have wanted to escape via route B. But where had he come from?

As you may know, an Orang-Outang exactly fitting this description disappeared from the Gibraltar Zoo in 1936. In 1943, only seven years later, a heavily-built 'man', wearing a boiler suit and thought at the time to have been the Prime Minister, stepped off an RAF Mosquito *en route* from Gibraltar, refused to speak to Military Personnel at Lyneham, Wilts RAF Station – I was there – and ran off into the night. The mystery has never been explained.

Until now. But what of the 'brace and bit'? I must confess that this baffled me for some considerable time. Then it hit me. Orang-Outangs are known to be prone to a type of parasite closely akin to the tapeworm. It seems probable that our friend, in his excitement at seizing the Woodpecker, engaged as it was in its boring activities, felt the need to loosen its bowels. It appears the tape-worm prevented this. Luckily, however, for the Orang-Outang, the tapeworm chose some moment, seconds later, to take leave of its host, and falling on the ground, formed the impression I mistakenly took for a type of drill. Later, in search of a new host, the worm no doubt wriggled away to some quiet spot where it could lie in wait for its intended victim. The mystery dissolved, and the last piece of the jigsaw fitted snugly into place. I have circulated a description of the Orang-Outang to all stations in the area, and to all airfields and ports.

R. Stoneley
Inspector.

EXCERPT FROM THE INTIMATE JOURNAL OF ROSE HOPKINS

Barry got to the top of my stockings tonight before he got his cramps. A big improvement on last night! To reach 'sweet sixteen' and never been touched! (I don't count Miss Brownlow.) It is too cruel. I am old, old, old! To feel the bud unfolding into the flower, but where is the sun? I wonder what it would be like with Barry? Barbara Bachelor says it is enormous, but he told me he's only got to think of something rude and he gets his cramps, so I don't see how she could know.

How I long to submit utterly! Phyllis and I were walking in Maniac's Dell this afternoon and we saw one of these Holes. At once I felt a strange stirring. The savagery of it!!! There were bits of bark and pieces of wood scattered round in all directions. The tree looked blissfully happy, though it must have been PAINFUL. Saw smashing see-thru nightie in British Home Stores. Don't think that the Bustaid Ointment is working. Still only thirty-two expanded. Damn.

EXCERPT FROM THE DIARY OF HUMPHREY MACKEVOY

I must protect Mummy from all this! Dr Phillips says that her blood pressure is already critical. What she needs is an atmosphere of security and peace, shielded from all excitement. Easier said than done! I was just changing the dressing on it this morning when Mummy's shrill cries told me that all was not well. I was paralysed with indecision. There was a long way to go with the bandage, but to have unwound it would have been madness. Tying a loose bow I buttoned my trousers and rushed downstairs. Mummy was lying in the hall in a pool of sunlight. I tried to lift her but she was too heavy. I was looking around for a lever when mercifully she came to.

At first she was confused, then the memory of some horror returned and she screamed again, pointing at the garden. I followed her pointing finger with my eyes, and what I saw chilled my stomach to its depths. It was a horrible sight. A Council employee, a small shrunken man in a cloth cap, was standing on the front lawn, unscrewing the lid of a large red drum. I was only wearing my fawn woollen cardigan and sandals, but I went out to confront him as I was. He had connected his pump to the barrel, and was advancing on the old *laburnum anagyriodes* that has stood in the corner of the garden since before Daddy went away.

I threw myself at him from behind, locking my forearm round his throat and bending him over backwards until we lost our balance and both fell to the ground. I knelt clumsily astride his chest, pinioning his arms to the ground. 'Get out! Get out !' I shouted, my hands at his throat, a red rage giving me a courage I never suspected I had. He knew he was beaten. His small bloodshot eyes looked wildly about for some way of escape, his mouth working convulsively under his pepper and salt moustache. 'I'm an epileptic,' he groaned, 'put a cork between my teeth or I'll bite my tongue off.' 'That's your problem,' I shouted, inwardly dreading that my mother might leave the house, dragging her slow way to my assistance, trip over the spraying apparatus and fall headlong on top of us, which would have been more than I could bear. 'My trees, you ruffian! Is nothing sacred?' I released my grip on his throat, got up and with almost superhuman strength carried his apparatus out through the gate and dropped it in the gutter.

When I returned he was getting up, wiping traces of foam from the sides of his mouth and fingering his throat. 'I was only acting on orders, guv'nor,' he told me, 'I don't like this any more than what you do. But look at this tree. How would you like to see this nice tree with a dirty great hole bored in it?' For the first time in a week I felt my loins quiver. Despite the constriction of the bandage I was aware of my manhood stirring awake like a sleepy lion. I had known the tree all my life. Every spring I had seen its blossoms hanging in golden chains, every autumn I had watched its nakedness emerging from its russet petticoat. It was almost a member of the family. Snig, the dog, was buried beneath it. But now its smooth slender trunk sent shivers of anticipation down my thighs.

I was stirred from my reverie by the man returning, dragging his apparatus and whistling an old song, 'You always hurt the one you love...' He pointed the head of his spray-gun at my tree. 'Now then, guv, be reasonable. It'll be over in a second.' Aware now of a calmer courage, I turned to face him, my buttocks brushing the bark. 'Spray my tree,' I whispered in a level voice, 'and you must spray me!' 'Sod it then,' he remarked, 'I've got my quota to think of,' and grumbling to himself he dragged the drum and the spray-gun out across the lawn and along behind the hedge to Mrs Peacock's. Turning, I embraced the tree, tears blinding my eyes, and laid my cheek against it, praying for darkness to fall.

LETTER FROM MONSIGNOR EVELYN HENNESSY TO THE
Mundham Advertiser

Dear Sir, I have been following with as much attention as the burdens of my office permit the controversy surrounding the so-called 'Mundham Borings'. Archdeacon Horns will, I know, forgive me if I express some scepticism about his sanity.

With the most oecumenical will in the world I cannot allow his admittedly inventive paleontology to go unchallenged. If his mental state permits it, may I suggest that he turn to Vol. XVII of Herrschel & Doenitz's authoritative *Mille Passu Sub Mare*? There he will find the sabre-toothed dormouse exploded once and for all. He would also find, on pp 9, 104 ff, a rational explanation for the Mundham phenomenon. The culprit, Sir, is the Screw-Headed Gasteropod, *Lumpus indivisibilis*, a horny-skinned worm-like mammal about the thickness of a man's thigh, with a single hooded eye in the top of its rounded proboscis. It moves, in sudden thrusting leaps with the aid of its gauzy wings, and figures large in the embroideries of the Blessed Catherine of Viterbo, the fourteenth-century visionary and patron of the painter Jaculum the Magnificent.

I remain, Yours etc,
E. Hennessy, S J.
Convent of St Victor Sylvester,
Reading.

EXCERPT FROM THE DIARY OF HUMPHREY MACKEVOY

The thought of that laburnum through the long twilight sent thrills through me more disturbing and more delicious (because more forbidden?) than the thought of any tree I have known these twenty-odd years. My hand shook over the baked beans as I prepared Mummy's supper on the gas stove. Only the acrid smell of the charred toast roused me from my dreams, and my distracted snatching of the kettle from the flame long before it had boiled made me curse softly as the dry leaves of the Camomile tea floated to the surface of the pot. I tied one of Mummy's long aprons round me to conceal my excitement and, stooping slightly, carried the Benares brass tray into Mummy's snuggery.

The confinement of the sickroom had never oppressed me more. The scent of Laxative Chocolate and Sloan's Liniment was almost drowned in the smell of Mummy's old flesh, whose wrinkled surface in the yellow circle of light thrown by the bedside lamp was revealed through the interstices of her pink crocheted bed jacket. She was reading Rochester's Complete Works again, and the diamond rings on her shaking fingers blurred in an erratic glitter, catching the light from the bedside lamp and so blinding me with their spectral blues and reds that I almost dropped the tray.

Her lips champed softly on her toothless gums, shaking the old webs of wrinkled skin that sagged at the corners of her mouth, and in the jellied depths of her spectacles a red tracery of blood vessels overlaid the one distorted opalescent globe, lit as if from within by the lamp at her side. In the other the grey cataract hung magnified like a sheep's lung in a butcher's shop. The hairdresser had been during the afternoon, and her mauve, stiff-lacquered hair concealed in its flawless draperies the lumpy baldness beneath. Miraculously, three inches of grey ash clung to the

22

wet cigarette that bobbed on her bristled chin, refusing to fall, like so much ash before it, into the mottled purple darkness below.

As I set the tray down on the quilted grey eiderdown I felt my bandaged member wilt in the foul air, the gauze loosening and slipping as it did so. Then the thought of the laburnum, standing alone and waiting in the cold dusk outside sent a stab of longing through my stomach and I turned aside to retch. How grateful I was in that moment for Mummy's deafness. The hot, stale air in the room stifled me. The dark mahogany wardrobe that Daddy brought back from Srinagar bulged towards me in this foetid, breathless compost that filled the whole room to the low nicotine-stained, shadow-haunted ceiling. I put down a hand to steady myself and sank to the wrist in the afternoon's bedpan.

'Butter the toast, darling, will you?' Mummy's words brought me back to my senses. How I hated myself for thinking of her in that cruel way! I wiped my fingers on her ruffled silk tea-gown that hung over the end of the bed, and complied with her request. I only half listened to the pit-a-pat of baked beans as she laboured to tamp them down into her mouth, for I was aware of other things stirring below. Aroused perhaps by the brushing contact with the polished walnut veneer of the bed, my manhood shifted and grew weighty, its dark ballast tanks filling for a long journey. A miraculous sense of freedom and health surrounded the erectile tissue, and it bucked with careless vigour against the rough tweed of my trousers.

Something of this must have betrayed itself in my face, for I was aware of Mummy's kindly eye quizzically gazing at me. 'Hump,' she breathed, 'you've gone very red.' 'It's your eye, Mother…the blood pressure.' I moved round the bed, stooping to conceal my jutting apron, and patted her pillows. Among the fur of her bolsters her Pekingese farted. Although she could not hear, Mummy was quick to notice this, and waving her copy of Rochester before her face she cursed the beans roundly. I apologized. She handed me the book and settled herself on the pillows, her beringed hands folded on her stomach.

As I read, the book propped in my lap, my lips forming the words mechanically, not listening to their sense, I marvelled at my own pent-up natural force. Pulsing through this interminable countdown like a moonrocket on its floodlit pad. Smoking with liquid oxygen, twinkling with tiny lights, ready at the touch of a button to rise thundering into the black ebony of the night. How long, O Lord, how long? One impatient twitch sent the book spiralling, and as I bent, with difficulty, to retrieve it, I saw that Mummy's thick eyelids were drooping behind her spectacles.

> Reason, an *ignis fatuus* of the Mind,
> Which leaves the Light of Nature, Sense, behind,
> Pathless and dangerous, wand'ring ways its takes
> Through Errours, fenny Bogs and thorny Brakes...

A moist snore told me that my work was done. On tiptoe and with a shudder, I removed her spectacles, and laid them on the marble top of the bedside table, extinguishing the light. Then I gave my straining penis its head and was drawn unresisting from the room.

Within moments I had snatched my drill from the darkness of the workshop and was quietly closing the back door. The frigid October air was wet on my cheeks, but I breathed it to the bottom of my lungs and then, casting caution to the winds, snatched at my flies and felt the incursion of coldness that flowed beneath the scrotum like Alpine currents lifting a balloon above the frozen peaks, or like the cold draught in a furnace that drives the glowing coal into a flame. For flame it was! My shoes broke through the crust of frost into the muddy fecundity of the lawn as I hurried to my tryst. The silhouette of my tree rose before me, its bare upper branches lit by a sodium light. Shielding it from my rampant anticipation and the silver drill that hung loose in my right hand, I pressed my cheek to its smooth bark, letting my left hand do reckless things about the bole. Somewhere above me a sleepy bird pushed its head further under its wing and ruffled its feathers.

Lasciviously I turned my face, brushing the cold bark with my lips, and began to explore its texture with my tongue. And you couldn't stop me, my laburnum, you with your branches pinioned in the air, leaving your trunk so bare, so bare, so unprotected, so vulnerable... How well you know me, slender laburnum. You who witnessed my first unsteady steps, felt my first innocent embraces! Shall I call you mother? Sister? Aunt, or Nurse? Nanny! Nanny Laburnum, how you have suffered. My tongue found a coy declivity, '*labiae laburni*'... Bruised by my cricket balls, pierced by my penknife thrown from a distance, and once I remember tattooed with my initials with a glowing skewer....

The drill sank, bit, turned, spewed, reversed and fell with a dull clank on the grass. I took a pace backwards, looked up into the tangle of bare branches, fingers extended to touch the bark, and launched myself, homing to the target like a missile. My telemetry was exact. Through the cork and the green outer bark, through the bast and the cambium, through the summer wood to the spring wood... I felt my member bathed in pale sunlight, lapped by the murmuring of doves, gilded by a thousand yellow crocuses, primrosed and honeysuckled, ransomed, healed, restored, forgiven. Now, at you! My filthy whore! Bitch, I'll split you! Beating my forehead to my own plunging rhythm I felt the bark break beneath my fingernails. So! You're giving in! On the fringes of my consciousness a bird squawked and fluttered out of the dark branches. My teeth sank into the bitter-tasting bark. I clenched my buttocks and felt the life surge from my feet, past my knees, to be poured out into that ravaged sanctum, the earliest growth-ring.

Silence rushed in at me from every horizon and I hung trembling.

It was cold in the afterglow. The sweat was chill in the hair on the back of my thighs. My trousers lay about my ankles. I could feel the bruises on my forehead swelling. But a sweet relief flooded me as I realized that I was whole again. My member hung limp, bathed in peace and spring's benison, tingling with well-being. A late dog pattered along the pavement beyond the privet hedge. It was old Spot, Mrs Beckett's black and white mongrel, pausing to sniff and cock a leg at the ash-bins by the Peacocks' back gate, and then trotting off into the night. A yellow oblong appeared at the window of the Peacocks' upstairs toilet, casting a pale patch of light on the lawn that touched the white shaft of my leg. I moved into the darkness, stooping to pull my trousers up, and heard the dwindling parididdles of Mrs Peacock's chronic cystitis. And my heart leapt at the sound, for I was free and whole and clean. Mrs Peacock's tight cough, and then the clank and the cascading flush...

I peeped in at Mummy before I went to bed. She was asleep with her mouth open, and I smiled to see my old bandage lying on the carpet like a winding-sheet in an abandoned tomb. I picked it up and tiptoed to the Aga. The threads of gauze grew red and a flame kindled. Miraculously healed, I looked in wonder at the flame, and then replaced the heavy iron lid. I fell asleep murmuring 'Labby, labby, labby', and smiling like a child.

EXCERPT FROM THE INTIMATE JOURNAL OF ROSE HOPKINS

Phyllis and I were in Maniac's Dell again. She is thinking of having it with little Charlie Sharples. She showed me some of his stuff on her hankie. I got my own back later when we saw a man hiding behind a tree. Phyllis said sometimes they pull it right out, so we went a bit nearer. I dared Phyllis to show her knickers. Guess what! It turned out to be an old Inspector!!! He was looking at one of the Holes that I had the dream about.* I said I know who did that and he's done it to me too. Phyllis turned bright red and the Inspector was amazed!!! I had to go to the Police Station. I said a man with a red sports car did it that looked a bit like Omar Sharif. What fibs!

The best bit was when they got this very young doctor to come who looked a bit like Richard Chamberlain only with glasses and he made me take my knickers down. We were alone in the room. He put on some plastic gloves. I was in heaven as he touched my thighs. Then he made a funny noise and sat down, holding his tummy. Afterwards he was very cross, but I am sure he didn't mean it. He has got my address and phone no. If only I had been wearing my new knickers that Barry gave me! I am going to tell Barry EVERYTHING!

LETTER TO MRS MACKEVOY FROM MRS BEATRICE GROSS

My dear Mrs Mackevoy,

Bless you for the travelling rug. You honestly shouldn't have bothered to have it cleaned! I've never seen 17th-century needlework come up so well after being 'retexed'.

What a 'fun' weekend it was! The boys can't *wait* to play table tennis with you again. Did you hear our *petit scandale*?

---

* I can find no reference to this dream in the Journal. H.M.

It's *too* riveting. After you'd gone Nat was out in the garden tying up the mums when he saw that that *lovely* Tree of Heaven by the conservatory had been got at by those beastly woodpeckers.

I asked little Stoneley, the Inspector, round to have a look at it – you know I can't *bear* that Mr Smart from the Council – and do you know, it's just as well! He's awfully coy about it, but there was something to do with footprints and what he called 'monkey business'! *Too* dramatic! Nat said he was going to take his gun to whatever it was, but for the last three nights the Cherry Brandy has got the better of him and poor yours truly has been *absolutely* terrified trying to get the gun off him in the middle of the night!

Do come over next weekend, though. Jack de Manio's coming down and I know he'd *adore* to meet you! Can Hump come too?

Love,
Bee (Gross).

P.S. The boys want to know if you could bring your ice skates.

EXCERPT FROM THE MUNDHAM ADVERTISER

Leaves From My Notebook
by
Midge Brownlow

What a bore those woodpeckers were! We're all heaving huge sighs of relief now that they seem to have gone, aren't we, and wasn't it strange the way they suddenly came and suddenly went. As I said to a friend, it was as if they were messengers, bringing news of disquiet and dark alarms to our little township.

Last Tuesday night, for example, Alderman Strangeways, who happens to be my nextdoor neighbour, found his ashbins overturned before the refuse collectors had a chance to empty them. The following afternoon his little daughter Linda — a delightful little girl with the eyes of a Gainsborough! — told me that she had heard funny sawing noises on the roof in the middle of the night.

Furthermore I hear that on Wednesday Town Clerk Chas Smart was the victim of really senseless vandalism. Lucy, his Schnauzer bitch, returned home with her back legs tied together with string, and as if this wasn't enough, hooligans poured some kind of paint-remover over his fine pair of garden statues, leaving the gnomes with an unpleasant flaky appearance. What next, one wonders?

While I'm on the woodpeckers, have you heard about the proposed Tree Defence League? Miss Longridge, who will need no introduction to Mundham nature lovers, very kindly came round this morning to explain it all to me. I expect we're all a bit uneasy about the use of what the experts call toxic pesticides, and particularly about the wholesale spraying of our lovely trees. Miss Longridge is determined to stop it. As she put it, every bird has an inalienable right to sit down, and I

must say I go along with her! Letters
and offers of support, please, to Miss
Ethne Longridge, OM, DSO and Bar,
'The Nest', Strawberry Lane,
Mundham. So long for now, Pen Pals,
back next week!

LETTER FROM MR CHAS SMART TO ALDERMAN STRANGEWAYS*

I must say I would not have expected even a [pig] like you
to stoop to tying a dog's legs together. How would you [like
it]? The police have been informed, and it will give me a
great deal of pleasure to see you [in the dock]. AS for your
mother...‡

LETTER TO MR HUMPHREY MACKEVOY FROM MISS ETHNE
LONGRIDGE, OM, DSO AND BAR

Dear Mr Mackevoy,
I'm sure you don't know me, but I have been into the
shop once or twice. I'm the bird woman!
Forgive an old fogey's enthusiasm but I've just heard
about the splendid stand you put up on behalf of your
garden, and I did want to slap you on the back. You may
have heard of the Tree Defence League, which I've started.
Could you find it in your heart to join us? We're very thin
on the ground at the moment, I'm afraid, but as I am sure
you will agree 'great oaks from tiny acorns grow'!
Do let me know your reaction, or better still, come and
have tea at the Nest!
                    Yours in haste, Ethne Longridge.

* I have taken considerable liberties with the lacunae in this
manuscript, which bears all the marks of rough treatment and
partial burning. H.M.
‡ The manuscript is not decipherable after this point. H.M.

P.S. Do you, by the wildest stretch of the imagination, have a duplicator? E.L.

POSTCARD, 5 $^{1}/_{2}''$ X 3 $^{1}/_{2}''$. ON THE OBVERSE A REPRODUCTION OF MUNCH'S 'THE SCREAM'. TO MRS BEATRICE GROSS FROM HUMPHREY MACKEVOY

Dear Mrs Gross,

Mother has asked me to reply to your kind invitation as she finds it difficult to move her fingers. Of course we'd love to come. Mr de Manio is a thrill! Mother talks of nothing else.

Sorry to hear about the tree. I remember it distinctly. I'm sure Inspector Stoneley will get to the bottom of it. Perhaps I could help Nat keep watch. Mother says could you remind Mrs Pritchett about the rubber sheet as it will save her work in the long run. We look forward to seeing you on Saturday.

Yours sincerely,

H. Mackevoy.

EXCERPT FROM THE DIARY OF HUMPHREY MACKEVOY

All my adult life I have dreaded the police knocking at the door in the night. Since I saw Bee's letter to Mummy I have been unable to sleep for the thought of it. Every morning on the way to work I pass young Bob Makins, proud as Punch in his new uniform, and I cannot see his round pink face and friendly blue eyes without thinking of the cold reproach that one day I may see in them. To be bundled into the back of a police car with Bob, who I have known since he was a lad! I lie awake at two or three in the morning, sweating with fear. Labby is my only comfort. It has been raining all the week, and tonight, as I found myself sobbing on its trunk, drops fell from the bare branches like cold tears, a nanny's tears who has been brutally used, but who still forgives me.

I am amazed at the health of my restored organ. Twice tonight and three times last night I have struggled into my overcoat, scarf and wellingtons, and gone to that sweet place and banisher of fear. The first clumsiness of passion has disappeared, and an almost domestic routine has taken its place. The prelude is longer and more intimate. I wander along the familiar paths of pleasure, recognizing with serenity the well-loved scars, cracks and swellings in the bark, the angle of a slender branch, the new spaces between the dead leaves where winter has brought the stars much closer. I never hurry now. The entry is muted and gentle, like the first bars of the *Magic Flute*. I have never loved a tree like this before: each nerve in my abdomen is strung to its highest pitch, yet each obeys the conductor's baton, melting and blending in the controlled, slow, certain crescendo.

Back in my bedroom, fear touches my spine once again. It would kill Mummy. When I failed my Army Medical, she couldn't face the neighbours for a month. Sitting at the table here, surrounded by my bits and pieces – it's better than just lying there, listening to a late car or the first milk float – I ought to feel quite safe. But even here I feel hunted. I have discovered that fear is like hunger: it deprives me of the ability to think, to plan, to act, to organize. I see my wet overcoat on the back of the door, and I know that there is a temporary escape.

A bedside table overturned in Mummy's restless sleep sounds enough like a knock on the front door to set my heart hammering. The house is still again, and I have to go out. But am I not using love as an anaesthetic, and how long can I hide in dreams?

EXCERPT FROM THE *Mundham Advertiser*

Disaster at Alderman's House

Family Flee as Roof Collapses

Lendoris, Kimberley Drive home of Councillor and Mrs Len Strangeways, was the venue for detachments of Mundham's Police Force and Fire Brigade early this morning after the alarm had been raised by a '999' call from a nearby kiosk.

Head and Torso

According to eye-witness reports, at approximately 1.30 a.m. there was a 'tearing crash' as a section of Alderman Strangeways' roof collapsed into the building. Speaking to an *Advertiser* reporter later this morning, a badly shaken Alderman Strangeways – he is 46 and Honorary Parks Superintendent – wore multiple bandages around his head and torso, and expressed what he called 'a burning sense of outrage' at what had happened.

Enquiry

Following last night's accident, which Alderman Strangeways believes to have been the work of a 'mad vandal', Police have ordered an enquiry to be carried out, under the chairmanship of Mr Chas Smart, the Town Clerk. Said

Mr Smart, 'We shall be looking most
closely into the standards of building
work employed in the Alderman's
home.' Lendoris was built in 1951 by
the firm of Building Contractors
Hooper and Strangeways.

EXCERPT FROM THE INTIMATE JOURNAL OF ROSE HOPKINS

I haven't been wicked for three nights now and am feeling
much better. I wonder if that's why Aunt Bertha went deaf
in the end? I got so fidgety in class today that Miss
Brownlow sent me outside. I AM IN LOVE!!!!! His name is
H.M. and he is very mature. He came to the school today
with some books for Mr Dalziel in the woodwork shop, and
saw me standing outside the classroom. I am sure he
noticed me. I couldn't look him in the face, but what a
bulge!! I've been thinking about it for hours. I gave Linda
Strangeways a bar of Cadbury's Flake to tell me his name.
Do not think she suspects. He is tall with dark hair and long
white fingers. He looks tired, as though he does it a lot, with
bags under his bedroom eyes. From his mouth I think he
could be CRUEL. Bought new hairbrush in Woolworth's.
It's bigger than my old one and stays cold. I am going to
write to H.M. tomorrow and send him the drawing Barry
did when he looked up my legs. Barry will be FURIOUS!

LETTER FROM HUMPHREY MACKEVOY TO MISS ETHNE
LONGRIDGE

Dear Miss Longridge,
Thank you for your kind letter. Of course I know who
you are, and am flattered that you should ask me to help in
such a worthy cause.

Unfortunately I have to go away this weekend, but if I could come to tea on Monday, D.V., I would be happy to bring my old Roneo and some skins.

                    Yours sincerely,

                    H. Mackevoy.

LETTER FROM MRS DORIS STRANGEWAYS TO DR PHILLIPS

Dear Doctor,

A matter has arisen which my husband feels shy about coming to see you with. As you know we have been married for seventeen years, and have always enjoyed our relations in the normal way.

As you may have heard our roof fell in recently and since then we have had Mr Smart's builders in. Last Saturday night Len was paying me his usual visit as per normal when, to cut a long story short, the bed broke. This seems incredible to me as neither of us is on the heavy side and the bed was still under guarantee. We weren't on the floor before we heard an alarm bell ringing like the ones shops have and Len nearly went spare trying to turn it off. We found it underneath the floorboards. Linda our daughter was most shocked.

As an upshot Len is not the man he was. He says that every time he as much as thinks about conjugal relations he gets all nervy and dreads something happening. Is there anything that can be done?

                    Yours truly,

                    D. Strangeways (Mrs)

LETTER FROM MR CHAS SMART TO ALDERMAN STRANGEWAYS

Dear Mr Strangeways,

How sad I was to hear of your terrible cave-in. My Department will be sending a full report in due course, and I hope that it will reveal no breach in the building regulations.

These must be trying times, coming on top, as they do, of your drastic cut-backs at Hooper's Birdoff where I gather numerous operatives have been obliged to return to the Domestic Burgundy side of the sheds, if any clear distinction can be made between the two products.

Signor F. Guillonotti joins me in sending our sympathies to a worthy competitor.

Cordially yours,

C. Smart.

P.S. You will not be surprised to learn of the death of our Schnauzer, Lucy, run over by an unknown driver under cover of night. My wife and I have always hated this dog and only kept it for appearances. Thank you very much. Similarly for the wanton strangling of our son's hamsters. One good turn deserves another…

EXCERT FROM THE *Indiana Journal of Ornithology*, VOL LVII, NO 36, pp 403 ff.

> Turning for a moment from the rigors of defoliation in the South East Asian Theater, we learn from a source in London Eng, for an exciting sighting in the Buckinghamshire sector. Midway between centuries-old Oxford and 'the Smoke' of capital London's urban sprawl lies Mundham,

a small market town mentioned in the Doomsday Book (1140). It was here, recently, that local birdbuffs glimpsed the extremely rare Fringed Woodpecker (*Gecinus Fimbreatus*) rating 4 dodos on the Indiana Scale. Reported enthusiast Mrs Townsend (49), a Mundham home-maker, 'its fringe was the colour of Instant Mashed Potato'. We await verification from Britain's Royal Ornithological Society.

LETTER FROM MR AND MRS GROSS TO JACK DE MANIO

Dear Mr de Manio,

Nat and I were *so* sorry that you couldn't manage the weekend, but we *absolutely* understood about the Polo Match with H.R.H. Don't worry a *bit* about not phoning until eleven -we never eat dinner until very late anyway – and in a way we were rather relieved because our party was somewhat overshadowed by one of our elderly guests having a haemorrhage.

And after that, to cap it all, we had quite a hoo-ha with the police! Who said small towns were dull? We *adored* the old man with no teeth who sang 'Some day I'll find you' this morning. Was he *really* ninety-three? By the way, if you should think of doing anything about Mundham, we really have the *rummest* customers you've ever come across.

If ever you *should* see the Templeton-Baineses again, do please give them our love. Carry on the wonderful work – since Winnie died there's no one like you!

Nat joins me in sending our best wishes,

Ever your fervent admirer,

Beatrice Gross.

EXCERPT FROM THE DIARY OF HUMPHREY MACKEVOY

Last night was one of the most terrible nights of my life. I had said goodbye to Labby just as it was getting light in a mood of optimistic exhaustion. Surely Bee couldn't be so callous as to know and to invite me to walk into a trap! And if there were only suspicions surely by offering to wait up with Nat I must have allayed them. I would be cheerful, relaxed and confident. I chose my lovat tweed suit with the flap on the breast pocket, a mustard tie and my old Veldschoen polished to a dim brilliance. I forced myself to whistle going down to breakfast, but my insouciance was short-lived.

Mummy had spent a restless night, dreaming that Jack de Manio was sparring with a punchbag on the lawn. She was very agitated, I'm afraid, and twice during breakfast I had to change her cushion. I calmed her as best I could, and after an infuriating wait for Mr Mason's taxi we finally set off for Bars at half past ten. After lunch Mummy was inveigled into a rough game of Cowboys and Indians with the boys, in the course of which she unfortunately fell on Jonathan, the youngest, who had to be put to bed, as did Mummy.

But there was no rest for me. As soon as Mummy was safely tucked up, Bee got me into the conservatory and brought the conversation round to the tree. I did my best to be amused, or shocked, or whatever she wanted me to be, but she couldn't let it rest there. I was dragged out to look at it, forced to examine the faint traces of my own bare footprints in the crumbling winter soil, pegged round with white tape. The official scrutiny which this implied terrified me, and then, as I was staring blankly at the sweet-jagged hole, crudely ringed with chalk, Bee slid the knife between my ribs, casually remarking that the Inspector was coming in after dinner.

I cannot remember anything between then and eight o'clock. All the interim was as a hideous dream. Mother woke at six, shouting for Jack de Manio, but he hadn't arrived. My sweating fingers fumbled at the Sisyphus task of fastening the hundred hooks and eyes of her orange lace evening dress: no sooner was it fastened across the back than it gave lower down, or vice versa, and I had to begin again. And yet there was something so comforting and dear about the scent of Johnson's Baby Powder and Mummy's familiar murmuring as she tried to ease on her long black gloves! I wanted to throw my arms round her and sob out my hideous story. But she was becoming impatient.

As we walked downstairs I was sure that the strain would prove too much for me. Sweat was running out of my hair, making my clean collar limp and clammy. The backs of my hands prickled with cold nausea. I mechanically picked up the roller skate on the stairs, helped Mummy down into the sofa, and handed round the Sherry as I normally do. My hands were shaking, but the jingling of the glasses on Nat's tray more than concealed my own clumsiness. I sat on the edge of my chair and felt the pit opening beneath me.

It was ten o'clock when Bee rang the BBC and left a message for Mr de Manio to call her back. By this time I was a little drunk. I looked round the room at Nat sneaking whisky into his sherry glass, Mummy dabbing at her eyes with a moist handkerchief and crooning softly to herself in her disappointment, and Bee, whose lipstick I realized for the first time lapped her nostrils: why should I feel so frightened about being taken away from this? Let the Inspector come. I looked out of the window and saw beyond my own distorted reflection my lofty Tree of Heaven, lit by the light in the boys' room upstairs, aloof, serene and utterly desirable.

At ten-thirty Bee was forced to admit defeat, and we sat

down to what remained of the lobster bisque and the cauliflower soufflé. Nat permitted himself a few spiked words about the empty chair on Bee's right, which I could see Mummy was taking very badly, and then went on, as usual, to praise the quality of the wine and retell the story of how he bought the Augustus John behind his head. It was in the middle of this that Mummy's nose began to bleed. None of us noticed it for a while, not even Mummy, but by the time the baked fish came in there was no mistaking it. The little tear-stained handkerchief was soon saturated, as was her serviette, mine and Nat's. There was nothing left but to take her upstairs to the bathroom.

With both taps in the wash-basin running, I did not at first hear the telephone ring. When I did the old panic returned. I turned them off, and roughly told Mummy to stop moaning and sit absolutely still, her head thrown back on the chair. Straining my ears in the silence I reasoned, in my sherry-certain state, that it must be the police, and they were bringing reinforcements. I could either escape or stay. The question was settled by Bee's irritated shout 'He's not coming!' A gargling groan escaped Mummy's lips, but I felt only relief. I was in the clear. Putting Mummy's head between her knees – easier said than done – I walked back to the head of the stairs.

Imagine my horror when I saw a pair of uniformed legs and heard the gruff voice apologizing for being late.

There was no going back. I steadied myself, one hand gripping the banister – my heart beating wildly – and began to walk down the white-carpeted stairs, defiant words forming in my mind. Implausibly, the Inspector laughed, raising his whisky glass and swaying slightly, his peaked cap under one arm. 'Talk about giving me a shock, Sir,' he roared, 'for a moment I thought you were our friend the orang-outang himself!'

The story was told soon enough, a wild fantastic hypothesis, in which the Inspector seemed to believe implicitly. Something about an ape, a grass snake, Gibraltar, measurements and samples of wood – the theories exploded about me like dizzy fireworks and I splashed in my innocence, exulting like a baby in a bath.

We sat round the fire for a long time, quite forgetting about Jack de Manio, and, I regret to say, Mummy, who woke with a start after midnight and managed to put herself to bed. It was after two when the Inspector left, and Bee and I had carried Nat upstairs. It seemed hours more before Bee turned out the lights and I heard the key turning in the lock of her bedroom door. Then, quiet as a mouse and ponderous as a bull, I crept to my pleasure. There were no shouts to stop me, no arresting hands on my shoulder, no shrilling of whistles or flash of gunfire from Nat's bedroom window, just the slow relentless rhythm in the darkness and a faint chorus of snores.

LETTER FROM SIGNOR F. GUILLONOTTI TO MR CHAS SMART

My dear Charlie,

I have had intelligence from our brother in Torino there is two days that the shipments will be arrive end of the month indicated as customary on invoice 'Fratelli Botelli Estratto di Pomodoro Qualita Super Extra'. The plant in Palermo is worked as you say flat out to the bust. Hooray! Commission as customary safe with Friends in Zurich.

May the Blessed St Anthony protect you and your divine babies.

Your loving brother in the law,

Francesco.

LETTER FROM CHAS SMART TO SIGNOR F. GUILLONOTTI

Dear Francesco,

Lovely to hear from you. All going on like a house on fire here. Seven-eighths of the municipal timber has been processed with a consumption of 7,000 gallons. As stocks are getting low the new shipment will be v. welcome.

You will appreciate however that the number of borough trees is not infinite. We have acted on Strangeways' tip and moved into private gardens, but this is running into local opposition. And without a return of the 'woodpecker' I cannot see my way clear to sanction a respraying in the municipal sector.

However, *caro mio*, don't let this get you down in the dumps. Failing any such return, my dear wife has come up with the idea of inducing a new epidemic by boring a few holes in conspicuous trees and thus inflaming public interest once again.

As the family joke has it, trust the Iciecreamioes to get you out of a jam. We're all booked up for Capri again in June, and Pia and I look forward to cracking a few bottles of Strega with you and yours. Remember the night Alberto fell in the harbour! We pray for you. May the Blessed Virgin watch over all your doings.

Affectionately,

Charlie.

LETTER FROM ROSE HOPKINS TO HUIMPHREY MACKEVOY, UNSIGNED

My Dearest Darling,

I am crazy for you. I cannot sleep for you. I am not a silly school girl. This is REAL!! If you love me too please don't be shy. We could meet after school in the Dell and I'll let you go all the way. Or we could do it at the back of the shop. Do you like this drawing? My boyfriend did it. Good job I'm wearing my knickers, isn't it?

I love you to Eternity,

B.O.M.B.A.Y.

What a lovely day! Even Mummy's bitter mood failed to dull the edge of my happiness and contentment. All day the sun shone small and golden in a sky of Botticelli blue.

I was up at six and couldn't resist saying good morning to Labby. It was still dark and I was very sleepy. Making love was almost like a dream. Indeed I think I must have dozed off, and woke still clinging to the trunk, woozily aware of a sound I could not identify at first. It was of course the hum and rattle of the Co-op milk float. Carelessly I smiled and experimented with a few slow strokes, pursuing a dreamy memory of some novel sensation half apprehended in sleep.

I lifted one foot and hooked my leg round the base of the trunk, slightly altering the angle of penetration. A moment later we were suddenly illuminated in the swing of the milkman's headlights. I froze and chuckled. For a second I was Jack Hawkins flattened against a wooden wall in some barbed-wire Stalag, weightless with arrogant laughter. I bit the bark to stifle my mirth, and the beam reversed, combing through the bare branches of the hedge into Albuhera Walk. I had to decide quickly whether to retreat or thrust home my attack. In the event the decision was made for me, and lifted by the base of the spine I was carried in a blinding delirium to a triumph more healing than laughter.

Afterwards I was the very pattern of cool efficiency. I withdrew, wiped, wrapped my dressing-gown round me and greeted Mr Partridge on the doorstep, and ordered a carton of cream as a treat for Mummy. And all this before dawn.

The sun was up by the time Mummy came down to breakfast. I made the mistake of turning on the wireless, and as luck would have it the first words that she heard were Mr de Manio's gruff interrogation of a publican whose tower of pennies for spastics had toppled and brained a guide dog. This was intolerable for Mummy, who the evening before, as we were leaving Bars, had forbidden me ever to mention Mr de Manio's name again. She turned off the wireless and attacked her boiled egg with such ferocity that the stem of the egg-cup snapped. From then on there was silence except for the obstinate crunching of dry toast.

I was relieved when the postman arrived, for in this mood Mummy is best left to herself. There was only one letter, and that a very curious and disagreeable one, written in a large immature hand on unpleasantly scented pink paper. It amounted to a declaration of love, and was unsigned. The envelope also contained, on a piece of thin, lined paper, a crude sketch in pencil of the sender's thighs and underwear. I hesitated between amusement and anxiety. Who could have sent it? I had seen nothing like it since school, and for a moment I felt the old familiar dread: then, feeling Mummy's eye on me, I managed to smile – Mummy's response was stony – and thrust it into my pocket.

Walking to work I dismissed the letter as a practical joke. A single man, living with one's mother, taking an antiquarian interest in books etc ... I was open to such malicious attacks.

It was a day that Thomas Traherne might have written of; a vision in which the commonplace houses and streets and gardens were plated with gold, and in which my heels rang and echoed on the pavement with loud confidence. For weeks I had been avoiding my old route to the shop, leading as it did past the plane tree that had caused me such distress. Today as I was walking down Grove Road I impulsively plunged right into Kimberley Drive and found myself as I strode past able to look with the calm of an old friend. I realized at that moment how deeply in love I was with Labby, and how proud I was of that love. A gang of builders were still busy on Councillor Strangeways' roof, and the smell of fresh tar and the sound of happy industry made the heart glad.

The morning passed in sunlit order. I gave Mrs Entwhistle far too much for a badly rubbed Curll Dunciad of 1742, reorganized the biographies, and at last unpacked the new Saul Bellow. I have never, since my childhood, lost my love of the smell of new books. There is a compact weight about a new book, the clean squareness of fresh-cut pages, the sharp fold of the dust-jacket, and the slight moistness of the deep-printed sheets that makes opening each page seem like hesitant intimacy with something virgin. I love my shop, too. Sitting in the little room at the back, with the bubbling gas fire and the old leather armchair, the roll-top desk and the coffee cups, I feel a donnish '*gemuetlichkeit*'.

I closed the shutters at four and carried my Roneo to Miss Longridge's as I had promised. What a splendid person she is! And how clever! I came away having promised to do much more than I had intended. We had tea, served by her companion, Miss Koch, from the most charming set of Blind Earl I have ever seen. She is very old now, and getting rather bald I'm afraid. Miss Koch flutters round her with cushions and shawls, and it is a pleasure to see with what grace these attentions are received. She is older than Mummy, of course, but with the persuasive skill of a Demosthenes. I find myself Secretary, Treasurer and Organizer of the Direct Action Committee. She is surprisingly familiar with the jargon of modern protest, no doubt because of her long years in the public service.

Her enthusiasm is most infectious, and no obstacle deters her. At one point in our conversation she gesticulated so violently with her walking stick that she shattered poor Miss Koch's spectacles. The unfortunate lady volunteered to walk to the hospital, and the incident in no way interrupted Miss Longridge's philippic against Mr Smart, spiced with sailors' oaths. I had no idea of the lengths to which his vile policies have been pursued, nor of his true motives in initiating them. I promised to take a soap-box to the park next Sunday morning and make the first public speech of my life. Miss Longridge is to compose a pamphlet which Miss Koch will type and duplicate, and we are to distribute them together.

So! Into politics! As I left the Nest - the latch of the garden gate clicked shut behind me - my imagination carried me shoulder-high towards the domination of ever greater crowds, stadiums, amphitheatres ... Nuremberg ... Peking: I heard the tense silence in the television studio before I calmly delivered the *coup de grâce* and saw the Prime Minister sink grovelling amid the sudden ruins of his political career; the screaming sirens, the motor-cycle escort, the black car hissing through wet streets at four in the morning towards the Palace: a hushed Commons, Downing Street, and then, at the weekend, Chequers. A regiment of soldiers to secure my privacy as I wandered naked through the woods, shrugging off the cares of office in a fine stand of old beeches.

Only day-dreams, of course, but I do believe everything is possible. I noticed this evening that I could see Labby's upper branches reaching up from as far away as Nethercott's Sweet Shop, and I felt what a sailor must feel seeing the spires of his home port. Coming into the garden I laid my hand on Labby's grey bark and brushed it with my lips. It was warm from the afternoon sun. Yes, with *love* everything is possible. *Amor vincit omnia.*

LETTER FROM INSPECTOR STONELY TO MISS ETHNE
LONGRIDGE, OM, DSO AND BAR

Dear Ethne,

Please pardon me for not replying to thank you for yours of the 5th inst, containing the information re. woodpeckers being the staple diet of the orang-outang.

The latter has led me a fine old dance, I must say. I have investigated alleged sightings as far afield as Winchelsea and Bristol. I began my enquiries full of hope following corroborated sightings around the Merrilees Home, but on closer investigation these proved to be no more than the figments of senile dementia. Either that or our old man of the woods is a quick-change artist and an adept at the art of pancake racing!

However to be serious, I haven't given up the search. The beast has laid low before. But rest assured I'll have him. Meanwhile the hunter is home from the hill and would esteem it a great honour to renew his acquaintance with you. Please put the Humper's Dingle incident out of your mind. The fires down below were banked many years back. Nowadays companionship means more to me than the seamy side.

I see the 'Seventh Seal' is on at the Regal. Would you be free to come and see it on Friday night? And perhaps partake of a spot of supper afterwards at the Copper Kettle.

Yours very truly,
Reggie.

LETTER FROM ROSE HOPKINS TO HUMHREY MACKEVOY,
UNSIGNED

My Dearest Darling Baby,

I long for you like the tunnel yearns for the train! I am
writing this lying on my bed, thinking of you. I am naked. I
followed you home from Miss Longridge's but you never
looked behind. I have put this letter you know where.
Forgive blot.

L.I.V.E.R.P.O.O.L.

EXCERPT FROM THE DIARY OF HUMPHREY MACKEVOY

I fear sometimes that Mummy is losing her mind. All this
week I have had scarcely a moment to myself. The trouble
began, I believe, with reading Kierkegaard, which I begged
her not to do, and was exacerbated by the de Manio
disappointment. On Tuesday morning I found her
downstairs before breakfast, playing patience with the tears
streaming down her cheeks. As I ate my cornflakes she told
me that she was not aware of any objective proof of her own
identity. I pointed out that if this were the case, my own
identity too was called into question. To my surprise she
accepted this. I told her not to be silly and to come and eat
her breakfast, and managed to turn the conversation to
ordering the new curtain material. I left her aimlessly
dipping toast in her boiled egg and spent the day without
giving the matter any further thought.

When I got back I saw at once that she was worse. She
told me she had sent Mrs Christie home and was still sitting
at the breakfast table with a far-away expression in her eye
and her jaws moving mechanically. I cannot bear to record
the endlessly repetitive arguments that we have had since
then, mostly on ostensibly philosophical and religious
topics. She keeps insisting that she was responsible for my

father's death. Since he died in an avalanche while working for the Post Office in India I find it hard to understand how this can be so: at the time she was looking after me here. But I have learned things about my father which I never knew. His ambition, for example, which drove him to sweat day after day in that rat-infested sorting office in Rawalpindi, where he was Mackevoy Sahib to that quaint band of bony, grave-eyed Pathans. Mummy showed me an old photograph and I was shocked at our physical resemblance, as I was at his obvious and terrible loneliness.

What had drawn him to the Himalayas no one knows. Mummy has told me that he always loathed heights and felt dizzy on a ladder. Yet whenever leave was given him he set off for the mountains, for the Roof of the World. Mummy still has postcards he sent from villages in the foothills, sepia pictures of monasteries, bright-tinted views of tea-plantations and snowy peaks. The look in his eyes, the uncanny similarity of our handwriting, and above all his secretiveness have made me melancholy and uneasy. He must have been the age I am now when he set out on that last walk. And this afternoon, sitting with Mummy in the front room in the gathering dusk, holding in my hand the view of the mountains where he was lost, I felt with an unaccustomed eeriness a direct connection between us.

As if Mummy's anxieties had not been enough, on Wednesday morning I received another of these stupid love letters, this one even more explicit than the last. For the last few days a plump schoolgirl has been leaning against Mrs Cameron's gatepost opposite and looking up at the house, but I cannot believe it could be her. The girl could be no more than fourteen. I suppose I should feel flattered.

I am terrified every time I think of standing up alone in the Park tomorrow. Miss Koch delivered the leaflets to the shop this morning, hardly recognizable under her bandages.

Seeing them there stacked on my desk suddenly made the whole thing horribly real, and although I am genuinely dedicated to the cause, I can't help hoping it will pour with rain tomorrow. I have had no time to write a speech – that is what I should be doing now – let alone rehearse. I just feel so desperately tired. Mummy has scarcely slept for a moment since Tuesday. On Wednesday night I waited until four o'clock before trying the back door, but Mummy heard me and screamed until I went to her, insisting that I was a burglar. Since then I have not dared to make love.

But if it were not for Labby – just seeing the tree there, slim and comfortable and grey in the morning, austere and peaceful at night – I could not go through with the speech tomorrow. And it's a *tree*! A solid, unbreathing, unmoving, unfeeling object. Mummy's speculations undermine the simplest assumptions. I will not question how my love arises or why: it is what sustains me. It is true, and I believe it to be true because it is impossible. In a way it's like Dad's mountains: after the struggle, giving myself entirely, I feel as he must have felt standing silent on a peak in Kashmir. A knowledge of harmony, of peace, and most of all of being most unassailably myself. Mummy's trouble may be that she has never had a mountain. I powdered a Welldorm into her camomile tea tonight and have taken away her Krafft-Ebing in the hope that she'll sleep. But I still daren't risk going into the garden. Oh Nanny, Labby, I'm still only a little boy: it's true, isn't it?

LETTER FROM MR CHAS SMART TO ALDERMAN STRANGEWAYS

The Grasslands Nursing Home,
Mundham.

Dear Mr Strangeways,

When a dozen magnums of sparkling rosé arrived at my front door with best wishes from an anonymous donor I might have known that someone disreputable in the wine trade was at the back of it.

However, as it was the eve of our Wedding Anniversary, I foolishly gave one a try. You know the result. My wife, Pia, is in the Infirmary and has had several transfusions, and my doctors fear that I may have to exist on a special roughage diet for several years to come.

If only I were not confined to this nursing home I would come over there and give you a taste of your own medicine. Meanwhile I lie here, planning.

> Yours etc,
>
> F. Nesbit.
> (Dictated by Alderman Smart but signed in his absence.)

MEMORANDUM FROM DETECTIVE–SUPERINTENDENT HOLLINSHED OF NEW SCOTLAND YARD TO SUPERINTENDENT ATKINS

Dear Tommy,

Pity you missed our little party at Virginia Water the other night. Flanagan's bag of films was exceptional and Betty and the girls gave us a slap-up evening.

Had a terrible head the next morning which wasn't made any better by your Stoneley. This Monkey Business has gone far enough. I have got more than enough on my plate without pestering the Home Office every day about fugitive apes.

Has it occurred to any of you down there that this Woodpecker Case might be a simple matter of malicious damage? Football supporters, Anarchists, students and so on. You'd be far better advised in my view to be checking on drill supplies than playing silly buggers with orang-outangs.

Having dinner with Barker at the Green Cockatoo in

Birmingham next Friday. Any chance of your coming over?
Don't do anything I wouldn't do.

Keep smiling,

Sam.

BROADSHEET PUBLISHED BY THE *Mundham Tree Defence League*

The Tree Defence League - The Facts!

During the last eight weeks Mundham has been privileged to play host to the very rare Fringed Woodpecker (*Gecinus Fimbreatus*). A beautiful creature and part of our ornithological heritage. The damage which this bird has inflicted on a very small number of trees in the area is minimal, and a tiny price to pay for the honour of having him here in our midst. The Council thinks otherwise. Thousands of gallons of corrosive bird-repellent have been sprayed willynilly on our trees, spelling doom not only to the Fringed Woodpecker but to many other feathered chums of longer standing. Already the Dawn Chorus is much diminished. When even the common sparrow is a rare sight it will be too late for action.

What You Can Do

1. Write to your MP.
2. Pester your local councillors, in particular the Town Clerk (telephone

number Mundham 413).

3. Prevent any of Mr Smart's operatives from entering private property. (Short of violence the law is on your side!)

4. Demand to know where the bird-repellent comes from, who manufactures it, and what it is made of.

5. Erect bird-tables and nesting boxes (no creosote please!) as alternative perching places.

6. Should you see the Fringed

Woodpecker (he looks like this:)
please telephone Miss Longridge (Mundham 327) immediately, DAY OR NIGHT!

7. Please give generously to the fighting fund. Be a friend to the Fringed Woodpecker! He has so many natural enemies!

THANK YOU

E.LONGRIDGE
H.MACKEVOY
U.KOCH
Organizing Committee.

LETTER FROM MRS BEATRICE GROSS TO MRS MACKEVOY

Dear Florence,

There's *absolutely* no need to torture yourself about what happened on Saturday night.* The boys enjoyed the weekend enormously. And don't worry about the washbasin, it's been broken for ages.

It's always such a joy to see you, and as I keep saying to Nat, if only we have a fraction of your *joie de vivre* when we are your age we shall count ourselves fortunate.

More dramas with the Police! It's *too* riveting. On Wednesday little Stoneley came round again - I can't remember whether you met him on Saturday night - this time with the Top Brass. A *frightfully* glamorous figure, simply covered with braid. Apparently Stoneley's got it all wrong and Glamourpants was hauling him over the coals like a Dutch Uncle.

Do come again soon. Nat's bought an enormous Dobermann Pinscher. I know he'll love you!

Yours ever,

Bee.

P.S. I'm sending back your cheque - don't be silly.

EXCERPT FROM THE MUNDHAM ADVERTISER

Wet Welcome for Tree League – Like Nazi Torture says Local Bookseller

Only a very small turnout greeted Mr H. Mackindoe of Glock and Sons the booksellers when he spoke in the Alderman Thornton Park on Sunday

* I can find no trace of my mother's letter to Mrs Gross. H.M.

morning on behalf of the newly-formed Tree League. Rain fell heavily throughout.

Nervous Start

Supported by Miss Ethne Longridge OM, DSO and Bar and Miss Elsie Cott, Mr Mackindoe made a nervous start with an unsympathetic audience but warmed to his theme and spoke emotionally against the Council's present spraying policy.

Himmler

'Mr Smart,' he said, 'is no better than a Himmler.' Innocent trees, he went on, were being treated like Nazi victims. If we had no respect for our trees, Mr Mackindoe said, how could we have respect for ourselves? Leaflets were distributed, and a collection taken. Said 91-year-old Miss Longridge, 'We are now considering Civil Disobedience.'

EXCERPT FROM THE DIARY OF HUMPHREY MACKEVOY

Oh God! An audience of five, three of them children, one reporter from the local newspaper and an elderly clergyman in a long yellow raincoat and carrying a set of golf-clubs. Despite Miss Longridge's enthusiastic introduction I know I spoke very poorly. One of the children started to heckle, and Miss Koch had to carry it away. I didn't know whether to look at the audience or not. I felt breathless, and a fat woman in the distance riding a bicycle and holding a red umbrella completely derailed my train of thought.

I had always thought of Mundham as having the atmosphere of early Rome, surrounded by seven hills: but in the winter light under the rain the wet roofs of the semi-detached houses, Bathgate's the butchers, Timms' the newsagents, the Town Guide by the telephone kiosk at the corner of Platts Lane all looked like a miserable transit camp of red brick and puddled asphalt, and my feeble oratory – in a cold panic I heard myself saying for the third time that trees were beautiful – seemed as banal and as lacking in distinction as the scene itself.

I tried to give meaning to what I was saying and encouraged by a few 'Hear! Hears!' from Miss Koch I managed to gain the attention of my audience by saying, however stiltedly and unnaturally, what I felt about Mr Smart. The clergyman, who was wiping the rain off his glasses with a handkerchief, put them on again and smiled at me. But even as I was aware of the concentration of their interest, I felt my own drifting again, and the sense of the triviality of the occasion made me heavy with despair. The cold rain was running down my neck. I looked across at Paradise Woods, hazy in the rain beyond the Golf Course, and I was filled with a desire to be there, alone and free and semi-nude among the tall wet trunks.

I finished haltingly. Miss Longridge and Miss Koch's boisterous applause was even less flattering than the silence of the little audience, who with the exception of the clergyman turned their backs and slouched away, feeling I suspect the disappointment of visitors cheated by a sideshow at a fair. The cleric, who introduced himself as Bishop Horns, squeezed my hand for a long time, patting it with the other and telling me about his own interest in fossils and the preservation of some kind of dormouse. He said, as far as I could gather, that he did not believe in the existence of the Fringed Woodpecker, but pledged his unstinting support.

Miss Koch ran after the audience, distributing pamphlets, and as we walked back across the Park Miss Longridge talked to the reporter about her future plans. I only wanted to go home, have a bath and try to forget it, but Miss Longridge insisted that I come back to the Nest for 'something warm'. Miss Koch took my cap and mac into the kitchen to dry, and I sat with the old lady on the William Morris sofa in front of the fire and sipped mulled vodka.

I began to apologize, but she brushed it aside with a gruff curse. There is something hypnotic about Ethne. I don't know whether it's her arthritic knuckles and pale translucent fingers weaving patterns in front of my face, her deep smoke-roughened voice, or simply her air of aristocratic confidence. She never believes that she can lose, and any woman who has silenced a machine gun nest and fixed mines to the keel of a pocket battleship has reason for such confidence!

After twenty minutes I could find no tenable objection to her plan. I am to chain myself to the sycamore outside the Town Hall before the next Council Meeting on Tuesday morning and the Press and Television are to be informed. I haven't dared tell Mummy. I can scarcely believe it myself. Mummy is rhythmically slamming the fridge door which means she wants me downstairs. If only I had a bit of time to think. I sometimes wonder whether I am going mad. I can't possibly go through with chaining myself to a tree. Me, of all people! Oh dear, there go the milk bottles! Will there never be a time when I can be myself? I haven't made love to Labby for six days... She's throwing dinner plates. I must go down.

EXCERPT FROM THE INTIMATE JOURNAL OF ROSE HOPKINS

I am going to jump in the river. He looks right through me. He'll be sorry when I am gone. They say that love's a word, a word I've only heard, but I will prove them wrong. I could not look at another man after H. Barry took it right out in RI but it left me cold. And anyway it is so weeny.

I shall wait till after the Sale at Dorothy Perkins, as I have been saving up four months for a Playtex Living Girdle, then I shall be able to go to the bridge in my emerald dance dress and my white tights and Saxone Ballerinas and just jump. It was just like Linda Strangeways' baby brother's.

LETTER FROM MISS ETHNE LONGRIDGE TO INSP STONELEY

My dear Reggie,

I haven't had a moment over the weekend to sit down and mull over the thrill of Friday night. Yes, Bergman is a genius! And you're such a good guide to his work. And isn't he a wonderful actor! When he came on in that great black hood I thought I was going to die. The sound of Swedish always reminds me of the greylag goose, and it brought back *such* memories of my Scandinavian trip before the '39 War. (Did you know Quisling once proposed to me?) Well, a million thanks for an enchanted reunion. The garlic bread at the Copper Kettle was a wonderful way to end an evening.

I hate to add a discordant note but I've thought and thought about your Chief's insane suspicions about Mr M, and the more I think the more ludicrous they are. Your theory is the correct one, Reggie, and it will be seen to be so. How could a man devote himself to the cause of *preserving* trees and at the same time be maliciously damaging them? What he will do this week will prove once and for all which side of the fence he is on!

I am, dear man, your affectionate friend,

Ethne.

EXCERPT FROM THE MUNDHAM POLICE LOG

In accordance with instructions I proceeded to the home of Mr and Mrs Nathaniel Gross and copied out a list of house guests from the Visitors' Book. List of persons included HRH The Duke of Windsor and Mrs Simpson, Sammy Davis Junior, the Maharajah of Jaipur, Mr Engelbert Humperdinck, the Duchess of Roxburghshire and Mr and Mrs F. Mackevoy. Telephone enquiries were made proving that all but the last named in the above list were fabrications. Under some pressure Mrs Gross signed a statement to this effect.

I proceeded therefore to 31, Albuhera Drive, to question Mrs Mackevoy, and rang the bell. I received no reply, although I heard sounds from the interior of the house consistent with the snoring of a large dog. On leaving the Mackevoy residence I observed that a tree in the south-east corner of the garden bore similar traces of boring or malicious damage to those noted in previous reports. Following Inspector Stoneley's instructions I immediately proceeded to position myself in the vicinity of Glock and Sons' Bookshop and commenced a close observation of Mr Mackevoy's movements. During later part of morning suspect was active in shop. At 11.00 a.m. he came to window and scrutinized the Alderman Thornton Park for several minutes. At 11.46 a.m. he left the premises, and went round corner to G. F. Barnet's Ironmongers' where he purchased a tin of 3-in-1 Oil price 4/7d. He then returned to the shop. I was relieved at 12.30 p.m. by Constable Mohammed.

LETTER FROM ALDERMAN STRANGEWAYS TO MR CHAS SMART

By Hand.

Dear Mr Smart,

Your letter left me dumbfounded. Your wife's drinking bouts are common knowledge: the Italians have a reputation for excess of every kind. And if you must join her in these drunken orgies then that is your own funeral. But it's no use trying to lay your gastric disorders at my door. It will not wash.

You can tell your wife, or 'Armpits' as we call her on the Council, to get back to her own dirty country, and stop annoying decent folk with her wine-sodden breath.

Doris and I had a good laugh over your cheap little trick with the fire alarm, I must say. I shall see you in the Council Chamber come Tuesday where we will carry through a censure motion against you. While you have been paying the price for your own swinish gluttony quite a few of the Councillors have come round to my way of thinking.

Your old friend,

Len.

EXCERPT FROM THE DIARY OF HUMPHREY MACKEVOY

How did I get myself into this mess? Miss Koch came over with the chains half an hour ago and I had to try them on. They are very heavy, and the manacles cut into my wrists. She also brought a large banner which she had painted in very uneven letters – the bandages on her eyes are still giving her trouble – THERE IS NOTHING LOVELIER THAN A TREE. It stands in the corner of my bedroom as I write, and it is infuriating how this crude legend has the power to awaken my body.

Mummy is very alarmed. Miss Koch had no sooner

helped me into the chains and snapped the padlock shut when Mummy shouted from the next room. I thoughtlessly clanked to the door. Mother's reaction was extreme panic. I rushed forward but this made it worse and Miss Koch's appearance in the doorway behind me momentarily unhinged her altogether. 'You shameless woman!' she shouted. 'How dare you practise such things in my house?' Miss Koch reeled under the imputation, and screaming herself ran from the house, slamming the front door.

I was now torn between comforting Mummy and following Miss Koch, for the key to the padlock was still in her hand. I could not possibly spend the night festooned in this way, so I forced Mummy back into the pillows, shouting at her to be quiet, and dragging the chains after me followed Miss Koch. She was halfway up Albuhera Drive before I caught up with her and persuaded her to unlock me. It was unfortunate that at this moment Bob Makins should pass, in uniform, on his 'beat'. I was very glad that we had known each other for such a long time, for otherwise the situation would have been hard to explain. On the face of it we must have seemed an odd couple. I myself weighed in chains, my companion's head in a turban of white bandages. As it was I gave Bob a bright smile and he went on his way.

Miss Koch was still sobbing as I sorted through the chains and shouldered them. We were standing in the penumbra of the street lamp outside Mrs Morrison's, and a stray branch from the old beech tree by her gate, still with a few brown leaves on it, tossed in the cold wind, making the shadows dance madly about us. I lent Miss Koch my handkerchief and she blew her nose. Then she said, in broken English, 'Your mother is unforgivable. She called me a prostitute. I am a German refugee and a virgin and I love you so much it gives me a pain.' My reaction was instinctive. No one had ever spoken to me like that before, and my experience of women had been confined really to Mummy. I dropped the chains and ran for my life.

Mummy was in a sulk when I got back. Not so much, it appeared, because of the fright she had had, but because in her view I had deserted her for Miss Koch. I patiently explained the purpose of the chains, and, with less conviction, Miss Koch's role in the enterprise. Her profession of love came back into my mind, and as I automatically answered Mummy's questions about the League, Miss Longridge, her furniture and general way of life, I wondered if Miss Koch might have written the anonymous letters. Or could it have been Miss Longridge herself? The more I thought of it, the more sure I became that these two ladies were using me for some humiliating purpose of their own. I resolved to have no more part in it, and told Mummy that I had changed my mind. To my tremendous surprise she would have none of it, and insisted with an impressive strength and firmness that to back out would be to dishonour the Mackevoy name. She was proud of me, and made me fetch our leaflet. Having read it she scrambled out of bed displaying an agility I had not seen since Mrs Peacock's elkhound went berserk. Within a quarter of an hour she had written to Mr Sieff, our MP, telephoned Mr Smart (mercifully without success), and dashed off a note to Miss Longridge, offering congratulations and suggesting various ways in which the campaign might develop. It was with the utmost difficulty that I dissuaded her from attending tomorrow's demonstration. At one point she even wanted to be chained up with me.

She is sitting up in bed now reading my own thumbed and stained edition of 'Trees of the British Isles'. From the wild look in her eyes I know that she will be awake all night. Bursts of delighted laughter and the shouted names of trees reach me now and then, and I know with equal certainty that for yet another night I shall be denied my Labby. At one moment I feel near tears of desperation, at the next I hear Mummy's ecstatic incantation of some of the most erotic words in the language - horse chestnut, silver beech, hornbeam - and a crowd of promiscuous images tumble pell-mell into my mind. Mummy will not be the only one who will not sleep tonight...

EXCERPT FROM THE MUNDHAM ADVERTISER

Voice of the Advertiser

Council Row Looms

Once again a row looms in the Council. Many Mundham residents are beginning to wonder why their elected representatives spend their time bickering amongst themselves instead of pulling together for the common weal.

The *Advertiser* has always taken an impartial stand and will continue to do so. But we say this. There appears to be some truth in Alderman Strangeways' privately expressed misgivings that the Town Clerk, Mr Chas Smart, has been overstepping his brief in the matter of the recent sprayings.

Huge quantities of bird repellent have been ordered from Italy and used on our trees despite every indication that the Woodpeckers have passed on. Let Mr Smart and his Italian-born wife ponder this. Public life in Great

Britain calls for the highest standards of probity and uprightness. He should issue a statement that will dispel rumours, otherwise a call for his resignation at this morning's Council Meeting will not fall on deaf ears.

We are informed that in addition to this dramatic clash, the newly-formed Tree Defence League is to stage a spectacular demonstration-style protest. Never let it be said that Mundham doesn't keep up with the times!

Talking of Alderman Len, it is a pleasure to congratulate him on the successful evening of domestic wine tasting held at the Hooper Strangeways Queen Elizabeth Cellars on Saturday night, attended by all our local 'big-wigs'. The occasion proved, once and for all, that when it comes to body, bouquet and flavour our English wines can knock spots off their expensively priced French and Italian rivals – any day of the week.

Well done, Len! Cheers!

EXCERPT FROM THE MUNDHAM POLICE LOG

Following Constable Makins's report entered above* the activities of the suspect Mackevoy and his companion have been brought to the attention of the Vice Squad. Pending

* This related, from a very different standpoint, substantially the events that I have described in my diary. H.M.

charges being preferred the observation and surveillance of the suspects has been made my own responsibility and I have drafted Constables O'Brien, Percy, Scroop and Pearmain to join Makins and Mohammed on the job.

At 8.30 a.m. on November 4th the woman, believed to be Miss U. Koch, of the Nest, Strawberry Lane, Mundham, returned to the Mackevoy residence carrying the chains and appliances described above. The door was opened by Mrs Mackevoy wearing the same olive green tracksuit in which she had been observed earlier by Makins exercising with Indian Clubs on the lawn. At approximately 9.30 a.m. Mrs Mackevoy embraced Miss Koch warmly and was heard to remark emphatically 'Forgive me, forgive me'. The two suspects then made their way to the Town Hall to take part in a public demonstration under the auspices of Miss Longridge, for which Police Permission has been granted. (See Correspondence under 'Longridge'.)

LETTER FROM ARCHDEACON (BISHOP) HORNS TO HUMPHREY MACKEVOY

Dear Mr Macintosh,

Your stirring words ring still in my mind, and I am writing to inform you that as yet no documentary evidence of the death of Himmler exists.

South America has been mentioned as a possible hideaway for this most unchristian of men, but I beg to differ. The Rhineland village of Mundheim (pop. 836) whose monastery dates back to the ninth century and owes its foundation to St Chrysistom the Glutton, sits like a saxophone case on a crag above the Lorelei-echoing waters, and it was here in the early twenties that Himmler spent his happiest years.

Where else would you expect a conscience-stricken ex-slave-master to make for in order to pray away his old age? But one must not underestimate Himmler's intelligence. He would never go to the obvious place. So one is back again in the dark night of speculation. Until one looks at Mr Smart! I take no credit for this leap of reason. It was your simile that struck the spark. I have but blown upon the flame. I have sent a copy of this letter to the Director of Public Prosecutions and the Prime Minister of Israel.

Yours in the Lord,

Thomas of Mundham.

EXCERPT FROM THE DIARY OF HUMPHREY MACKEVOY

Only the last hour has purged away the pent-up misery of a morning on the rack. In this state of stolen fulfilment the humiliating events of this morning and the follies of this afternoon are like monsters in a dream, lunging and snapping at me. I am sitting at my table with a cold compress round my loins. Drips from it fall intermittently into the enamel bucket beneath my basket chair and my bruised flesh passes scandalous pictures to my brain. I must impose an order on this lewdly beckoning chaos. I will begin at the beginning.

At about ten this morning Miss Koch chained me to a sycamore which I would judge to be about forty years old. I stood with my back to the trunk, and a chain was passed through the manacles on my wrists, securing my hands at either side of the tree. A second chain was passed three times round my body and through my legs, then padlocked. The placards were arranged around me and Miss Koch took her place on a canvas stool at my side. Directly opposite me across the pavement was the main entrance to the Town Hall.

I was wearing my fawn mac, leather gauntlets, and my green Kangol hat – a Christmas present from Mummy.

Miss Longridge had insisted on conducting operations from the Nest, providing Miss Koch with an American cloth bag containing a Thermos flask of coffee and egg sandwiches, and I was therefore left to satisfy the cynical curiosity of the boy from the *Advertiser* who sniffed his way through a few ill-informed questions. The first hour passed in acute embarrassment. Miss Koch would not speak to me and passers-by pretended not to see me.

Shortly after eleven the first Councillors began to arrive. No one paid much attention to me, except the Mayor, Mr Cotton, who jovially compared his chain of office to my own, nudging me in the ribs and giving me his famous 'thumbs up' sign before climbing the steps to have his photograph taken. Mr Strangeways was cheered into the Town Hall by a group of women-employees, I suspect, let off for the day from his bottling plant. The last to arrive was Mr Smart, looking pale and walking gingerly with a stick.

He was the first to show any sign of anger at our demonstration. He came up, and stooping down with some difficulty grabbed a handful of earth, gravel and matchsticks from the base of the tree, and rubbed it into my face. He then stood back, smiling, and said, 'If I lose this vote today, Sonny Jim, I'll have your bleeding guts for garters.' Miss Koch replied, as I was spitting out dirt, with a flood of German which none of us could understand, and Mr Smart was helped up the steps into the Town Hall.

The meeting lasted two and a quarter hours. Just before one o'clock Miss Koch opened the bag and unwrapped the egg sandwiches. Relations between us were still strained and formal after last night's emotional episode. I felt I had acted like a coward, and her physical presence unnerved me, a feeling that was intensified by my being chained; even the tree at my back, which pressed against my calves, my thighs, my shoulder-blades, gave me no erotic consolation. I was so tense in Miss Koch's presence that the touch of the bark was as dead as stone. She for her part seemed happily bemused by Mummy's overwhelming demonstration of vitality and affection, though still shy and inhibited, thank God, in her overtures to me.

Now, as she tried to feed me with the sandwiches and to give me sips of hot coffee from the Thermos, my physical discomfort gave way to impotent rage. It was not her fault that she kept missing my mouth with the scrambled egg sandwiches and coffee, but I had not realized how far the bandages impeded her vision. Worse, she refused to accept my curt assurances that I was not hungry and went on, with a distant smile of resignation, prodding food in the general direction of my mouth. My wrists jerked painfully against the manacles, and turning my head firmly away from her I felt the corner of a sandwich penetrate my ear. She was moistening her hankie with the tip of her tongue and about to dab at the corners of my mouth with it when Mr Smart appeared at the top of the steps, holding out the seat of his trousers and alone.

His progress down the steps was painful, and it was obvious that the vote had gone against him. He said nothing, but stared malevolently at me through his thick glasses. His car was brought round, and he was driven off, half-crouching in the back like some thick-spectacled orang-outang. He was followed shortly afterwards by a triumphant Strangeways, surrounded by back-slapping Councillors, and cheered by his employees still waiting on the pavement. Mr Ellis, who works in the archives at the Town Hall, came to speak to me. At first his words were faint and indistinct. I realized he was addressing the ear still blocked with scrambled egg. Moving round to the other side he told me that Smart had lost a vote of confidence by a large margin and that all further spraying was to be suspended.

Miss Koch shouted in triumph, scattering a golden shower of egg and breadcrumbs over Mr Ellis' stomach.

Had she been able to find the keys, the demonstration might have been accounted a total success. As it was I waited three quarters of an hour while she ransacked her clothing and went to telephone Miss Longridge before going back to the house for a duplicate set.

Left alone, an object of cursory interest to the lunchtime shoppers, I was glad when it began to rain. Soon the shining pavements were deserted and only an occasional car hissed past with windscreen-wipers thumping. I became aware that I was rhythmically flexing my buttocks against the bark, and closing my eyes I felt the rain splash on my face as I surrendered to visions of a sacred wood, an enchanted forest in which, like a Cluny tapestry, the slender trees grew so close together that my back might be caressed by one while another received the slow thrusts of my rich passion.

My reverie was interrupted when Miss Koch returned to release me, but even her proximity failed to soften my hard resolve to satisfy the voluptuous dream. The afternoon was passed amid scenes of heady self-congratulation. Mummy was summoned to the Nest. Miss Longridge was in a delirium of triumph, now demanding that we retell our story for the umpteenth time, now firing off telegrams to friends abroad, now striding to the wall-map of Mundham and banging her fist against the curving broad arrows of Mr Smart's spraying operations, suddenly dead and emptied of threat. Mummy was in tremendous form. Her new enthusiasm for life illuminated everything she did, and made even her infirmities beautiful. The afternoon sun played tricks among the tufts of down on her chin and her dull eye twinkled.

We all drank too much vodka. Mummy had us in fits with her stories of Frinton in the twenties, and Miss

Longridge painted such a picture of staying with Mussolini in Capri before the war that the very air in the room became redolent of garlic and gardenias and the sun-sparkling heat of the Mediterranean. Not to be outdone, Miss Koch, whose facial expression hovered between that of a sheep about to be slaughtered and a priest awaiting ordination, fetched down her zither and picked over the hesitant harmonies of some Bavarian peasant dance, yodelling without conviction. Mummy joined in an octave lower and soon the carpet bounced to a wine-treading polka with which Mummy proved herself surprisingly familiar, linking arms with Miss Longridge and endangering the fragile furniture as they swung round and round. Lying on the sofa I saw them as two Bacchae from Thebes, exulting in the death of Pentheus.

I thought of our trees, safe now from the murderous spray and ready for my own fierce homage. I thought of Labby, and the last time we had made love, over a week ago now. In my imagination, I caressed the grey bark and felt the safety of that well-worn orifice. But even as I did so the image eluded me, and darker thoughts interposed themselves, of that mediaeval wood, where I, a naked knight, was hung in thorny chains, trunks pressing on me. I had bored them all and could move from one to another in wild experiments of fresh couplings. My fingers lingered where my flesh had been.

Whether it was a sudden shift in my position I do not know, but the cushion I had placed on my lap was suddenly twitched on to the floor in the path of Miss Longridge's antic feet. She stumbled, and stretching out a hand to save herself, let down her full weight on the zither, which proved unexpectedly fragile. There was a cacophonous jangling chord, which was to be its last. At first Miss Koch did not notice what had happened. For a moment I pitied her, but the feeling was swamped by a gurgling tide of uncontrollable laughter. Mummy saw the funny side at once and Miss Longridge soon followed her, bringing her fist down on the shattered instrument and slapping Miss Koch on the shoulder.

I remember very little of the walk home with Mother, who insisted on stopping at Simons's off-licence and buying a bottle. When I woke up she was lying on the dining room table like a stranded walrus, and our festive bottle of Simons's Potato Stout was standing in a small, perfect circle of vomit, whether mine or hers it was impossible to tell, though she had taken the precaution of covering me with one of her rubber sheets, and this in itself suggested the latter. As I went through the long familiar routine of undressing her and levering her into bed, my own body ached like a lewd wreck, a charred lay figure with a mouthful of cinders, my eyeballs rolling in ash. Then my manhood rose like a phoenix, crowing silently in the enveloping dark.

Looking out of Mummy's window I saw two policemen who I did not recognize on the other side of the road. I could see Labby, branches lifted to the twilight, silvery trunk bare, innocent and trusting, and I realized that our tryst would be delayed. I drew the curtains and tiptoed upstairs to my bedroom. In the bottom left-hand drawer of my dressing table was my drill, which I had not used for weeks. I don't know what made me open it, but as I lifted the brass handles I saw that my fingers were trembling. A Pandora's box! I couldn't resist, and, as I knew they would, winged phantoms galloped the night-roads of my blood. To be unfaithful! Feverishly I took out the drill, kissing the shank and oiling the bit with my tongue until I found between my lips a fragment of Labby's virginity. I tasted its tastelessness and, in an access of deliberate sacrilege, forced myself to swallow it. Why should I have wanted to sully my love, degrade it, soil it? And yet I did. Just the sight of the drill sent me wild with desire.

I crossed the landing to the front bedroom and went to the window. The policemen were still deep in conversation, and as I turned to look at Labby a cruel smile formed on my lips. The way over the back wall was one I had often used as a child, and there was an easy drop on the other side into a mound built up by the bodies of cats I had shot with my airgun from point-blank range. It was dark now, and I made my way through the back lanes until I came to the pumping station. There, by the side of the reservoir, grew a copse planted in 1946 of slender young birch.

On the reservoir side a chill wind was making the water slap against the bank, and I surprised a mallard. A few torn clouds drove across the moon, destroying for a moment the shadows of my seraglio. Then it gleamed again, round and white, revealing the whole length of the reservoir, the rustling tufts of grass at my feet and the pale limbs of the birches. Why had I never come here before? In defiance of the night wind I tore off my clothes, and saw with an ancient delight the shadow of my manhood etched upon the grass. I shook it with a wild joy, laughing up at the moon, and threw myself down on my back.

From here I looked along a curved colonnade of pale trees following the line of the shore. Those nearest I could reach out and touch, and I rolled over moaning with pleasure, and took up the drill, turning back to trace my initials on the bole of the nearest tree. Suddenly my heart contracted with a shock. I saw, only six inches from the ground, a hole that I myself could have made. For a moment the physical dimensions of a person who might have used such a hole carried me into the land of Grimm's Fairy Tales, and I half expected to see Snow White herself gliding between the trees. I got to my feet and immediately saw on the next tree a second hole, this time at eye level. All reason fled. I drew back aghast, knowing that on my secret island I had company.

But my body overcame my mind, and I fled the confusion in the moonlit wood. I slapped the bare trunks, flaunting my body wantonly against their shy flanks. 'You want it, I've got it!' I hissed, and began to make obscene passes with the glinting drill. It was as though the trees had been theatrically arranged for my pleasure. Each held an identical fascination, each pulled me towards it, and I stood for a moment at the centre of a magic circle, suspended in the perfect balance of their magnetic attractions. To move, to have one, would be to lose the others, and I wanted them all!

Then, as if I had been there a thousand times, a thousand years ago, I turned my head and saw, some twenty yards away, not one but two lovelies, close together, growing as if from the same root, contemplating, reflecting each other in what I imagined in the moonlight to be the silent rapture of mutual love. Softly I stalked them. My body was washed in the cold moonlight and striped by the shadows of the branches. The soles of my feet were numb to the chill leaf mould, and the breath of the night air against that hottest part of me delicately prefigured a denser envelopment. Growling in my throat I loped forward, stepping between them as one mounts a lady's bicycle.

Exulting, I was wedged in the embrace of those Narcissus twins, even my manhood pressed flat against my stomach, while my buttocks were gently parted. An indescribable sensation! I had interrupted their double gaze, I had trespassed on that adoring space. I laughed. I was in the driving seat now! What was a dull tree in the corner of a suburban garden to this! I brought the drill to the ready. Unhappily there was no room to use it, and though miserable at the thought of having to vacate this tandem bliss, even for a moment, I slipped out and began the cruel operation. What texture! What colour! What bouquet! I withdrew the drill with such force that the wooden butt thudded back against the virgin twin, bruising its bark and leaving a shallow depression.

O divine promiscuity! What dull sublunary love I had known till now. On pavements, and amid the din of cities, assignations in public parks as conventional as taking the dog for a walk on Sunday mornings. Even the Tree of Heaven for all its subtle enigmatic charm, seemed like the Taj Mahal seen before lunch from the windows of a charabanc. Now I was on my magic horse, riding through a starry firmament to the Source of Light. As I thrust forward my buttocks fell comfortably together, but as I withdrew with the same hot vigour they were forced roughly apart. Stray stanzas of Xenophon came into my mind: vivid images of those rude Greeks cutting through trunk after trunk, felling whole forests to build their mighty navies, leaving the land arid, bare and waterless beneath the pitiless Doric sky.

My climax came with a swiftness that astonished me. Used to the slow rowing of the boat to the other shore, the squeak of the lightly-oiled rowlocks, the pleasurable resting on the oars, this sudden speedboat hydroplaning through my veins left me breathless. I was amazed at my own virility. While the watching trees still seemed to whirl round me in a giddy roundabout, silently begging for their turn, I retrieved the drill and turning my back on my seeping damage I rammed the bit into the tender bruise. The difference between them was astonishing. Grown up together, nurtured by the same sun, the same soil, and yet how miraculously unique they both were!

This was soft where the other had been hard; the arrangement of its internal knots applied pressures that made me giggle as they diverted me, pinched me and sent me stubbing up blind alleys. High celeste discords of pain were added to the deep diapason of pleasure. My scarred foreskin shuttled and butted. A dirty thought crossed my mind. My bottom was already badly scratched by the jagged circumference of the hole at my back, but now I allowed my hand to squeeze between my buttock and the tree and slipped my index finger into that abandoned sweetheart. A few seconds of heavy petting, and a huge tea rose exploded in my mind. Surging like a tidal wave, the earth heaved and threw me.

Falling, falling, falling: a sudden jarring pain wrenched at my consciousness and then my shoulder hit the earth. How long I lay there I cannot say, but as awareness returned to my spreadeagled limbs, heralded by the ache of fresh bruises and the familiar sting of splinters, I felt I had gone a journey down the stars.

Now, sitting here, laved and swaddled and completely at peace, it is time to doff the poultices and to sleep.

EXCERPT FROM THE MUNDHAM POLICE STATION BEAT INFORMATION BOOK

Operation Jupiter:

At the afternoon (15.00 hrs) briefing of Tuesday November 4th Inspector Stoneley outlined the following objectives:

(1)   to co-ordinate surveillance;
(2)   to apprehend suspect if possible in the act of committing the felony;
(3)   bring same into custody with the minimum publicity.

EXCERPT FROM THE DIARY OF HUMPHREY MACKEVOY

I want to die. Why am I writing this? Because Mummy cannot bear any longer to hear me sobbing. And why am I sobbing? Because my Labby has been cut down. It is still out there, lying across the lawn. Last night follows me like the wrath of God, and my guilt obsesses me. I am so disgusted by my body that my skin seems alien, leprous, reptilian. I want to go and weep on Labby's trunk but it would be too dramatic a gesture. I am denied even the comfort of ritual. Everything is pointless and I feel like a murderer.

I must force myself to write it down, if only to pass the time.

I woke up with a headache this morning and had to spend rather a long time in the bathroom with the Germolene. How vile! Tenderly cosseting the tempter and deceiver! I could tear it out by the roots. Oh for the courage of Origen!

Mummy came in from her run and forked in eight underdone rashers of bacon and three eggs, a piece of liver she found in the larder and several thick slices of fried bread spread with marmalade. She seemed completely unaffected by yesterday's debauch – have I done nothing but wallow in filth all my life? – and prattled about our political triumph. Triumph? I feel like a man who has been in the grave for five days. I suppose I was already feeling guilty.

As I left the house I could not look at Labby. I felt the tree's reproof on my back, already stiffening from last night's bruises. My feeble pretence of looking in the opposite direction and waving good morning to Bob Makins was transparent. The simple truth was that I could not look Labby in the trunk. I sidled out of the gate, and against my normal practice began to walk down the road towards the Congregational Church. It sickens me to think that even then I was congratulating myself on having avoided a confrontation. A truant from my habitual way to work and from my love, I felt a silly exhilaration and even welcomed the lewd stirring of last night's memories.

At the shop my uneasiness returned. There were no customers, and I forced myself to be busy with sweeping and dusting. Tidying a drawer I found a fragment of a poem I once tried to write for Labby. I felt sick and hid it under some papers.

> 'Frail bark, anchored in Lethe
> with a cargo of sperm....'

Just after twelve a woman came into the shop dressed in mourning with a black veil. I had never seen her before. She said she was looking for 'a good laugh', and I sent her away with *The Wit of the Duke of Edinburgh*. But she disturbed me, and when she left I felt such pangs of guilt that I could not keep still. I decided to break the habit of years and have lunch at home. I wanted to re-establish, no matter how fleetingly, our relationship.

As I turned the corner by Nethercott's Sweet Shop I felt a shock of dread. Something was wrong and I was not sure what it was. In the first sick seconds of a nightmare I ran. It was only when I saw the unbroken line of the hedge that I knew for certain what had happened.

They had sawn through the trunk at an odd height. The upper branches almost reached the house. I stepped through the maze of sprung branches. The way the twigs quivered at my touch left me dumb in the face of this death. When I reached the stump I saw that they had made the cut exactly where we had made love so many times. The shallow channel was smooth and worn, the radius of a rough, white, saw-scarred circle. Two policemen had followed me into the garden, attracted perhaps by my involuntary shouts, and hearing the squeak of Mrs Peacock's lavatory window. I turned to see her malevolent gnomish face alight with '*schadenfreude*'. The policemen were facetious, and asked me whether 'The old woodpecker hadn't overdone it this time'. I said nothing. They watched me as I went into the house, and went off laughing.

Mummy was not at home. The Aga had gone out, and the house was unusually cold. I sat down in Mummy's armchair in the front room without bothering to move the newspaper that lay across it. A late fly buzzed feebly on its back on the windowsill, its legs busy as it turned slowly on the spot. The telephone rang, and answering it I heard a man say 'I warned you, Sonny Jim.'

I sat motionless all the afternoon, occasionally wondering where Mummy was and listening to the sporadic bangs of early fireworks. It was dark when I heard Mummy's voice singing the Woody Woodpecker's Song and returning the neighbours' insults. As she opened the gate I heard her swearing, and when she came into the room I could see that despite the effects of drink she had received a shock. Then, for the first time, I began to weep.

There had been a second celebration at the Nest, this time to mark the confirmation by the Royal Ornithological Society of Miss Longridge's sighting of the Fringed Woodpecker. More vodka had been drunk, and Miss Koch had cut her foot badly dancing on broken glass. Mummy chattered on, obviously trying to cheer me, while I sat weeping and trying to smile. She dismissed the cutting down of the laburnum as an act of petty revenge by Smart and suggested ways in which we could retaliate. I said there was no point. Finally my tears began to irritate her, and I came upstairs. So here I am again in the present, with nothing to protect me from myself.

Oh Labby! I would uproot every tree I saw in the wood last night if it would bring you back. Who would have thought that I would outlive you? And how will I bear next spring without seeing your leaf-buds, your golden chains? I have dreamed all this long winter of making love to you in those golden chains, and now . . . I must go out. I went out last night. Oh last night! When I could have been with Labby. I must forget. I think I shall kill myself. There is no alternative.

EXCERPT FROM THE INTIMATE JOURNAL OF ROSE HOPKINS

What a night! I was brought home in a Z Car. One of the detectives put his hand up my legs and let me feel his trousers. Then he got a tummy ache and had to stop.

It is all over with H.M. as far as I am concerned. He does it with trees. I saw him tonight and it is lovely and big. Much bigger than my detective's. But he is WARPED. I went round to his house tonight to see if I could see him undressing again* and he rushed past me. I followed him out to the Golf Course. I thought he was going to meet Old Foureyes‡ but she was not there. He went on up Kenilworth Lane and I managed to catch up with him. I showed him my knickers and told him I loved him but he went mad. Then he ran away. Then I ran after him and Old Foureyes came out of the bushes. She tried to grab hold of his thing but he pushed her in the chest and she fell down. Then he vanished in the trees. There was a gale blowing and I was only wearing my scanties. After a bit I saw him making a hole in a huge tree. Then he got it out and stuffed it in the hole. He was shouting and crying and I went up to ask him

* I can find no reference to this episode. H.M.

‡ I take this to refer to Miss Koch, who normally wore spectacles. H.M.

to do me next. But before I got there Old Foureyes ran in and tried to pull him out. Then the Police whistles went and they got hold of me. That was when I had the best look at it. My detective is going to take me for a ride in his car tomorrow in the evening. I hope the back seat is nice and roomy!!!!! I am going to borrow some of Mummy's FemFresh. Roll on tomorrow!

LETTER FROM MISS KOCH TO MISS ETHNE LONGRIDGE OM, DSO AND BAR

Dear Miss Longridge!

I feel I must offer to you an explanation why I have so suddenly left the Nest. I know that I am necessary to you, but Amor demands that I am with him who is everything to me.

My dear Patroness, do not judge me as he will be judged. The world is too full of sadness that we should need to increase it. He has done wrong I know, and offended against Nature, but I love him.

I was with him on this terrible night. The way was hard and my foot was swelling and gave me pain, but I followed. Fate it was that has brought him to where I was guarding the nightjars from the fireworks. What I saw this night will remain in my soul for ever. He came before me like a crucifixion of Gruenewald. It is us women who have done this to him in that we have not understood him. My dear Ethne, we are all guilty.

I am staying in Reading with his mother at the above address until his Trial. Mrs Gumbs who looks after us is very friendly and we are quite comfortable. Humphrey we will visit soon. Poor man, surely he has suffered enough.

Your very humble

Ursula Koch.

P.S. Mrs Mackevoy I know would send greetings, but she is gone out to make purchases.

EXCERPT FROM THE MUNDHAM POLICE STATION BEAT
INFORMATION BOOK

Operation Jupiter:

Following a call from Constable Mohammed at 20.30 hrs to the effect that suspect had left his residence openly carrying a brace and bit and in an agitated state, reinforcements were ordered to the vicinity of Paradise Woods, being the direction taken by the suspect.

At approximately 21.15 hours Constable Mohammed, shadowing at regulation distance, observed the suspect to accost a young girl and interfere with her clothing. Suspect then became nervous and ran off up Kenilworth Lane. At this point reinforcements joined Constable Mohammed and contact was briefly lost, the weather being inclement and a Force 8 gale blowing. However Constable Makins reported contact with female suspect Koch in the environs of Hollyhedge Farm and the operation switched its axis.

At 21.35 hrs Koch led reinforcements into small clearing A (see attached map), still unaware of pursuit, where suspect Mackevoy was in process of inflicting malicious damage on Norwegian Spruce B. Koch then attempted to restrain Mackevoy and reinforcements closed in. Turning from tree Mackevoy indecently exposed himself to all present. After being cautioned Mackevoy remarked 'Has it come to this? Oh Labby, Labby,' and broke down.

Detective Constable Pearmain then apprehended the young girl Rose Hopkins previously assaulted by Mackevoy who was wandering in the woods in a dazed condition. Charges on this offence will be preferred pending Police psychiatrist's report. The suspect Koch was released after questioning. Prisoner was transferred to Headquarters in Reading and remanded. Superintendent Atkins commended Inspector Stoneley and all involved for their prompt and efficient action.

Part Two

Eric has just brought me this paper and a choice of four brass nibs. It is wonderful to think that I have nothing to do until supper time. The food is plentiful, hot and good, and it is surprising how quickly one gets used to strong tea. The cell is warm, I have new blankets, and as I am on the side of the building away from the street there is very little noise from the traffic. In its simplicity and fine proportion the cell transcends any penal atmosphere and recalls rather the chaste interior of a Fra Angelico annunciation. My angel is Eric, with his metal-framed spectacles and neatly-clipped moustache, and instead of a lily he carries a bunch of keys.

I have not seen another prisoner since I arrived, the only human sounds are the conversations of the policemen on duty at the desk at the end of the corridor. Every hour Eric comes to see that I am still here and asks me if there is anything I need. I arrived too late to get to know the Constable on the night shift - his name is Brian and he has a Welsh accent. I am determined not to give way to self-pity. I find the sound of my pen on the paper very comforting, and I am happy to be able to write down the events of last night in such peace.

I was mad I think, really mad. I remember deciding that

life was intolerable and that I must kill myself. I realize now that I was dramatizing the situation in an attempt to give my chaotic life some final shape and significance. I think I went into the bathroom and opened my shirt to discover exactly where the heart lay, and marked it with a circle in Mummy's lipstick. Then I went to my bedroom and closed the door, imagining that I would never open it again. I decided that it would be appropriate to kill myself with the drill, without which none of my wicked infidelity of the night before would have been possible. But the action of taking the brace and bit out of the drawer brought back such a rush of associations that I felt the slack and wrinkled life-raft of my love grow buoyant.

What would Labby have wished me to do? To die like a trapped animal, or to go out blazing?

Before I knew it I was running down Albuhera Drive, brandishing my brace and bit like a flaming sword. Rockets raped the sky and bangers exploded behind the hedges. The air smelt of cordite and nests of serpents crackled among the treetops. I was blind to the ejaculations of the Roman Candles. My blue touchpaper was smouldering, and the world would be wise to stand clear.

Above the town a great wind rushed, and I flung away to its source. Half way up the Golf Course I looked back. Mundham was like a small town experiencing civil war. Somewhere a dog was howling, and explosions and bursting lights lifted the edges of the night. Behind me the great stands of Paradise Woods, my Dunsinane; a fortress labyrinthed – oh Labby, Labby! – with tunnels of lust. Already I could hear the gigantic creakings of boughs and trunks against the howling of the wind. This was my music, not the puny bangs of the cities of men. Paradise! To die of a surfeit of delight! I turned my back on Mundham and leaned on the wind.

In Kenilworth Lane I met the imbecile child. She rushed out of the hedge and said something I could not catch as her mouth was obscured by her skirt. The sight of her fat thighs and cheap underclothes was like a parody temptation to return to the city. I listened to her muffled interrogative shout once more and ran. Out of the frying pan into the fire! A second she-devil was sent to tempt me. Miss Koch's bandaged head loomed at me from a hollybush. Out she jumped and made to embrace me, but I pushed her aside and ran on through the tossing bushes.

Once I dropped my brace and bit, and half-weeping with frustration delved in a rabbit hole until I found it. The undergrowth snatched playfully at my flapping trousers, roots tripped and tumbled me, bare brambles blooded me till I was superb, arrogant in the darkness, ready for a giant. And a giant I found. Oh yes! Alone in a clearing, steepled like Strasburg Cathedral, a hundred-foot Norwegian Spruce, trying to free its roots from the earth, its branches heaving in a slow erotic dance that shuddered on the brink of ecstasy: wanting me, moaning in the gale, taunting me, daring me...I shouted my defiance at its rolling summit and ran in a mad charge beneath its tormented canopy.

Sink! Lean! Turn! A churning frenzy of splintering wood. My aim was a little high, but no matter: I'll have you on tiptoe, my proud tyrant! Fly gaped and flesh stood challenging. I attacked. At the first thrust I realized I had entered an iron maiden of splintery hell, but my valour turned those spikes to yielding flowerets as I fought among the dark blossoms. The golden nectar was guarded though: further in fresh perils awaited me. Yielding to the gale the massive trunk began to move, and I was in danger of being utterly crushed within the wood. But I was cunning and filled with a giddy courage. I would have my way. As the creaking timber leaned and the channel narrowed I tantalizingly withdrew, plunging home again through the terror-gates of wooden needles as I matched my rhythm to the wind. It was obvious who was master. I was crushing the flowers in my dangerous garden, pressing out the juices, breathing the death-heavy scent of forgetfulness, of poppy and asphodel when the woman Koch seized me by the waist and tried to pull me away. Dunderhead! My rhythm was destroyed. One puff of wind and I was a goner. In such circumstances it would have been madness to go on.

I left the tree and swung round with her still clinging to my back, and found myself face to face with Bob Makins and half a dozen colleagues. Strangely I was not surprised, or even embarrassed, only overwhelmed with boundless grief for my love. What followed was like a play at which I was only a spectator. Eric has just come in with my supper on a tray. Two plump sausages with chips, a bottle of Daddy's Sauce, a bowl of rice pudding and my mug of tea. He made me uneasy by telling me that tomorrow I am to have a visitor. But he did not know who it was. I must eat my supper before it gets cold.

EXCERPT FROM THE CELL BOOK, READING POLICE STATION

- 16.00: Quiet, writing.
- 17.00 : Quiet, still writing.
- 18.00: Supper. Requested tin of Germolene from Dispensary. I asked prisoner if he wished to see the doctor but he replied no, it was old trouble playing him up.
- 19.00: Delivered Germolene. Prisoner asked for a pair of tweezers. Lent him Sergeant Bull's.
- 20.00: Prisoner still applying Germolene to genital areas. Returned tweezers. Lights out.

Mundham Bookshop Blaze

Mr Humphrey Mackevoy, Secretary of the Tree Defence League, was not available for comment late on Wednesday night following a fire which gutted his business premises at Glock and Sons Ltd, the booksellers. It is believed the blaze was started by a firework. The fire was brought under control by the Fire Brigade following a 999 call.

Leaves From My Notebook
by
Midge Brownlow

Poor Mr Smart! They say it never rains but it pours, but down Mr Smart's way it's certainly coming down cats and dogs. On top of having to resign from his post as Town Clerk, he and his wife had to go to Hospital with food poisoning: and now, vandals have smashed all their windows, and not content with that, knocked the greenhouse down. To add insult to injury they have daubed obscenities all over the walls and roof.

He is not the only victim. When my nextdoor neighbour, Mr Strangeways, went to start his car the other morning, the engine exploded,* and only good

* This was reported in the previous issue of the paper but less concisely. A Sicilian, Ugo Spinellini, was later arrested and charged. H.M.

89

luck saved the Councillor from serious injury. Police are looking for an ice-cream man with a tricycle who was seen tinkering with the engine moments before.

This violence has gone far enough! Are we going to slip back into another Dark Age or not? Please, police, do something!

LETTER FROM MRS POLLOCK TO THE MUNDHAM SANITARY INSPECTOR

Dear Mr Wilcox,

I am writing to you as I have something unsanitary to report. My work is at the Strangeways Bottling Plant where I work on the bottle-filling machine. The reason I am writing to you in confidence is that I do not wish to be victimized. Mr Strangeways is a very hard man.

Last Tuesday I was alone in the Vat Room when a gentleman I did not recognize at the time came in and offered me two pounds if I would let him climb up the Main Vat as he was interested in wines. As you know my hubby, Gerald, was badly bitten by the rats in our Council Dwelling and we need the extra.

Anyway the gentleman climbed up the ladder, took down his trousers and did his number twos into the vat. Surely this can't be sanitary? I didn't feel right about bottling all day Wednesday. The gentleman concerned I have seen a lot in the town. He is walking with a stick just now and has glasses.

Yours truly,

F. C. Pollock (Mrs),
14, Hooper Drive,
Ringwood Estate.

I am very unhappy. While the door of my cell was locked I
was free, today it was opened and I am a prisoner again. At
half past nine this morning Eric came to say I had visitors.
Walking along the green-painted corridor to the visitors'
room I passed through air-pockets of unpleasant scent, and
knew that Miss Koch was in the offing. She was sitting on a
bench beside a fat, bald clergyman, who was wearing a
cassock and smoking a cigar. Eric asked the clergyman to
extinguish his cigar, to which he replied 'Bugger off'. The
voice was unmistakable. It was Mummy. Eric decided not to
hear Mummy's remark and took up his position by the
door.

Miss Koch got up. I could not look at Mummy, who was
introduced to me by Miss Koch as Father Savonarola, and
greeted me with a wide leer and a wink. Miss Koch herself
had taken off her bandages, allowing her blonde hair to fall
almost to her shoulders, and was plainly embarrassed. She
restrained herself from kissing me, for which I was grateful,
and we sat down. Mummy continued to grin, and when
Eric was looking at a photograph on the wall of a police
football team in order to give us more privacy, she hitched
up her cassock to show me a sturdy spade strapped to the
inside of her leg. Strapped to the other, I learned later, was a
crow-bar.

Conversation was impossible in the face of these
revelations. Even my own shame, which in more ordinary
circumstances would have made the interview painful, was
thrown into insignificance by Mother's crazy subterfuge.
While I urgently telegraphed my distaste for these
arrangements, Mother boomed on in a voice that should
not have deceived a six-year-old, let alone a skilled detector
of falsehood like Eric, only four feet away. Her inventions

were of the clumsiest, and as she mixed inelegant anecdotes
of parochial life with barely veiled stratagems for my escape,
Miss Koch coloured crimson and stared with fearful
intensity at her white-knuckled hands. I realized that my
mime was having no effect, and had to resort to shouting
her down, calling her 'Father' and indicating as violently as
I could that while I had been in prison I had lost my faith
and wished to have nothing further to do with the Church.
Miss Koch began to cry, and Eric gently announced that
our time was up.

Walking out into the corridor stiff-legged and sideways,
Mummy asked Eric if she could go to the lavatory, and
pushing open the door of the Ladies she disappeared.
There were two sharp clanks and she reappeared with her
arms and hands inside the cassock, the sleeves hanging
empty. She remarked on how cold it was in 'these prisons'
and asked to view my cell. Eric was clearly loath to refuse a
man of the cloth, even one who spoke indistinctly round a
badly-chewed dead cigar, and led the three of us here. Once
inside Mummy demanded to hear my confession, her voice
inexplicably shifting into stage Irish. Eric agreed to this,
despite my eye-rolling despair, and took Miss Koch out into
the corridor.

Left alone with mother I felt like a small boy again,
fidgety and trapped. I had gone over again and again in my
mind since Wednesday night, how I should explain my
perversion, what form this confession would take, and here
was Mummy, bald as a billiard ball, huge in her black
cassock and here was I kneeling before her. In that moment
the pantomime seemed appropriate. I looked up at the soft
hollows of her temples and for the first time marvelled at
her self-sacrifice. Tears came to my eyes, and I gripped the
stuff of her cassock that smelled of moth-balls. I whispered
'Mother, forgive me', and felt the fingers that were ruffling

my hair tug my head back to look at her.

From what she excitedly whispered it was clear that she did not believe what Miss Koch had told her. She was convinced that I was a victim of Mr Smart's vendetta (which of course I am) and talked wildly of 'springing' me – she had pushed the tools under my blankets – of having a hearse waiting at the kerb that evening, of driving to Auntie Vera's at King's Lynn with me in the coffin, of planning a terrible revenge on Smart involving a King Cobra and a ball of string. It was useless to argue with her. I rose and kissed her affectionately, and at the same moment Eric came and cleared his throat in the doorway. Mummy patted my cheek, walking into the corridor with affected unconcern, and striking a match on her heel to light another huge cigar. She offered one to Eric, but he refused.

I lay on my bed for some time after they had gone, painfully aware of the implements under the blanket. My serenity of yesterday has quite disappeared. The World has beaten a path to my cell. The same scenes that I remembered yesterday as though I had read about them in a history have become real again, and belonging to me. It is I who suffer. I who stood and looked at Labby's obscene death. I who stood humiliated like a rutting animal in front of Bob Makins. There is no escape from this history. What I thought was a monkish cell is a cage in the market place, and the distinction between public and private has been smashed.

I remember seeing a film once in which an actress said 'You can't keep running, Jake: you're not running away from the Law, you're running away from yourself.' How true that is. These tools that Mummy brought could manufacture only a false freedom: to give them up was imperative. I rattled the cell door and Eric came at once. I noticed a chilliness in his attitude to me, and he seemed at pains to avoid physical contact. Explanation was difficult. I said that I was not finding my bed at all comfortable, and pulling back the covers on the pretext that I believed there must be lumps in the mattress I blurted out something like 'I wonder how they got there!' and was immensely relieved when Eric proved as concerned as I pretended to be.

He immediately blamed it on someone called 'Barmy Gilpin', a cleaner who was apparently notorious for this kind of carelessness, and apologized to me. I asked him for some more paper, and before beginning my diary, sat down to write Mummy a cautionary note.*

LETTER FROM INSPECTOR STONELEY TO MISS ETHNE LONGRIDGE,OM,DSO AND BAR

My dear Ethne,

You were right to slap my face. I came straight home and had an ice-cold bath by way of remorse, which has given me a streaming cold. I haven't been slapped by a woman for donkey's years, and it fair set me thinking. I suppose the last person to do that was old Granny Butcher, the Sunday School teacher, and the only other woman I have ever loved. I say 'other', Ethne, on purpose.

Yes, you had every right to slap my face, I would never dispute that. Being a policeman isn't always a bed of roses. This Mackevoy business has got us all down. Poor chap. But you can't get away with that kind of twisted sex behaviour, or we'd all be up Queer Street. All the same I liked him, he was a friend of yours, and I'll do everything in my power to be of assistance to him.

---

* I have been unable to find this among Mummy's papers. I advised, as I remember, against the clerical disguise and any further attempts at rescue. H.M.

My cheek still smarts occasionally and it makes me think of you.

>Your loving friend,

>Reginald.

LETTER FROM ALDERMAN STRANGEWAYS TO MR CHAS SMART

Dear Mr Smart,

Once again, when I went out to pick up the newspaper this morning, I found more disgusting diarrhoea all over the porch. This has gone far enough. My wife is very delicate, and cannot face her food.

I am writing this to let you know that I have placed the matter in the hands of my solicitors.

>Yours etc,

>L. Strangeways.

EXCERPT FROM THE INTIMATE JOURNAL OF ROSE HOPKINS

I have made myself sore. I was so disappointed I could have banged my head against a wall, but I didn't. Men are so timid! Charlie Pearmain came up to school today in break in his Z Car and made me get in. Linda Strangeways was livid. If looks could kill! I took my knickers off but he said he was taking me to the doctor's and wouldn't do anything. When I felt his trousers he got narked and had indigestion. I think I must have overdone it with the Fem-Fresh.

I was looking forward to the doctor after the one that looked like Richard Chamberlain. But this one was old with a long white moustache. I got on the sofa and opened my legs as wide as I could but he got cross and said he was not that kind of doctor. All he wanted to do was ask a lot of stupid questions about H.M. I could see he knew I was telling fibs and I got mad. When the policewoman came to take me back to school I said the old doctor had put his hand up me but she slapped me round the head and said I was evil. If only I was! I hate men.

I saw Miss Brownlow after school and she wants to take me to a concert in Windsor. I think I might let her.

LETTER FROM MISS KOCH TO HUMPHREY MACKEVOY

My dear Humphrey!

Your worthy Mama has asked me that I should write to thank you for your dear letter. I have read it also and we have wept together a long time.

Of course we will not come again, if that is what you wish: of course your mother will no longer dress as a priest: of course you must plead that you are guilty if that is your desire. But that you are guilty in the deed your Mama cannot believe.

You say if we wish to disown you you will resign yourself to it: but oh Dearest Humphrey till all the seas are dry, my Dear, and the rocks melt in the heat of the sun, we shall be waiting. Be of good cheer! Your shop is burned down, so there is nothing left to fret about.

We both embrace you, My Dearest, we think of you day and night.

> Your Own,
>
> Ursula.

LETTER FROM MRS POLLOCK TO THE MUNDHAM SANITARY PSYCHIATRIST

Dear Sir,

I am sorry not to have had a reply to my previous letter of last Thursday, especially as the unsanitary incident I referred to has happened again. The gentleman concerned appeared again this afternoon, as white as a sheet, and offered me four pounds if I would help him up the ladder. I had to wait at the top of the vat with him until he had finished and could see the shocking effect on the wine. Surely this must be stopped? I know you are busy but please oblige. I enclose SAE & oblige.

     Yours Truly

     F. C. Pollock (Mrs),
     14, Hooper Drive,
     Ringwood Estate.

EXTRACT FROM A REPORT BY MR GRAHAM NIPPLE, CONSULTANT PSYCHIATRIST

I examined the prisoner on the 7th November. Mackevoy is 41 years old, and in good physical condition. He has never consulted a psychiatrist and was fully co-operative. He is intelligent, and has led a perfectly normal life, studying English at university and using a small legacy from his father, a Civil Servant, to buy a bookshop which he has run single-handed some 17 years. His relationship with his mother, who is still alive, is completely normal in every respect, and in free association games gave no hint of oedipal tendencies.

The most interesting aspect of his psychic life lies in the libido transference from women or men to any species of tree, though he singled out a laburnum in his garden for special attention. This form of totemism is relatively rare, and usually repressed due to the severe physical strain involved and social disapproval. This has not been the case here. Under light hypnosis I uncovered the prisoner's legs and suggested in him an infant state. From his babbling I gathered that the first word he learned to speak was 'colander'. Repetition of this word brought about erection and subsequent bed-wetting.

The patient became more than usually embarrassed on waking from the trance at this very common occurrence and I transcribe the following exchanges from my tape-recording of our interview. Eric Queensbury speaks first.

Constable:	Look out Sir!
Mackevoy:	Pop, pop...
Nipple:	Damn you to hell. Wake up you bastard! Look what you've done to my lounge suit.
Mackevoy:	Where am I? God, what's this?
Nipple:	There's nothing to worry about. You have been in a light trance, and experienced regression to infancy. In other words I've made you remember what it was like to be six months old. You did very well.
Mackevoy:	I'm soaking!
Nipple:	Calm yourself. Constable, bring the prisoner a towel.
Mackevoy:	You mad charlatan! Do you think you've proved anything by this disgusting practical joke? I know your sort. A hundred years ago you'd have been working in a fairground! Give me my trousers! Loon! Mountebank! Ughh!
Nipple:	Does it make you happy to insult me?
Mackevoy:	I can only pity the poor devils who are taken in by your kind. Honestly! You ought to have a bone through your nose, doing a rain dance. Look at this mattress!
Nipple:	Shut up!
Mackevoy:	You're not much to look at, are you? Little broken veins all over your nose,

hair growing out of your ears, and if
you're going to make anything of this
stupid career you might at least do
something about your breath!

This abuse continued in a predictable way for some
minutes. The outburst demonstrates the way in which the
tree obsession has produced a complementary inability to
deal with any normal social situation. The prisoner's
unbridled vehemence springs from a basic insecurity,
closely connected with his shame, which could result in
violence. My recommendation is that in this case treatment
by aversion therapy, drugs or analysis would be useless, and
now that frontal lobotomy is frowned on I would come
down in favour of nine months' hard labour.

LETTER FROM MRS BEATRICE GROSS TO MRS MACKEVOY

Dear Flo,

Nat was passing your door this morning and saw a
middle-aged couple sawing up a tree on your front lawn. He
went in and found you weren't at home. *Ghastly* people, Nat
said, apparently from next door: thought Nat was some sort
of burglar. Anyway, in the end they told him where you
were, and said they'd come to 'help'.

What are you doing in Reading? And where is
Humphrey? *Too* awful about his little shop! We heard
absolutely *filthy* rumours at a wine-tasting down at
Strangeways last night. They upset Nat *terribly*: he's been in
bed all day. I'm afraid I may be going down with the 'flu too.
What I want to say, Flo, is that if there is any truth in these
stories - and God knows, we've been through enough
misery because of it – you can always count on us.
Humphrey was always a bit odd, but it takes all sorts,
doesn't it.

Of course if there is any scandal we do have to think of Nat's position at the BBC. Poor darling, he's been trotting all night! Sorry, I had to break off there. One's body is a bore, isn't it? Please let us know the *moment* you get back. We can't *wait* to hear your news.

Must dash,

Bee.

LETTER FROM MISS ETHNE LONGRIDGE OM, DSO AND BAR TO INSPECTOR STONELEY

Dear naughty Reggie,

Golly, what fun it was! I've never heard the 'Mikado' so badly sung. Let's not talk again about the Mackevoy business, but do be tough with the people at Reading. I've sent three cables to the PM but I know how tied up he is in Africa. It's so miserably lonely here without Ursie.

You did understand, didn't you, why I couldn't kiss you last night, but the sole at the Copper Kettle is always a bit on the bony side and I was banking on getting back to the house for a rinse.

Wednesday night is a *must*. Strange how Bergman always crops up for us! Couldn't we stay at the Sparrow and Windlass afterwards and go on to Reading in the morning?

Your sweetheart,

Ethne.

EXCERPT FROM THE DIARY OF HUMPHREY MACKEVOY

Despite Eric's advice I have informed the Clerk of the Court that I intend to conduct my own defence. After that fool Nipple the thought of baring my soul to a solicitor makes me feel sick. There are three charges, only one of which I shall deny. Even Nipple could see that the idea of my interfering with the fat little harpy was too ludicrous to take seriously.

But Malicious Damage! Was the Spruce malicious? How could it be? A tree cannot be anything but what is, and that all the time. You may call it malicious, but then it remains so: malicious as seed, as sapling, in its maturity. Is it possible to say of me that I am malicious in the same way? That I am what I am because I cannot be otherwise? How then can I accept blame or guilt? The word 'malicious' is deprived of meaning. And that was true before I loved Labby. Since the whole function of my life was to have all trees, I was guiltless and blameless because what I did was natural. I did what I did because there was no alternative.

In loving Labby I made a choice no different in quality, no more moral than the 'choice' between tree and tree that I had made before: it was only a 'choice' in that by selecting Labby I was postponing intimacy with a host of other trees. But at that moment I knew that I had no alternative but to love Labby. Labby was my tree of knowledge. I recognized that to love Labby alone was my natural function. And with that recognition everything that had been natural became unnatural, what had been invitation became temptation: to yield was to do damage, not only to Labby, not only to myself, but to the other tree. It *was* malicious damage. And I see now that the damage I wrought that night by the reservoir was manifest in the damage of Labby's death. I am guilty.

As to the other charge of indecently exposing myself I am less certain. It was never my intention to do so. I did not expose myself to the world, the world exposed itself to me. And if you kick down a man's bathroom door you cannot complain if you find him naked. It is ironic that in bringing me into the Public Court to answer this charge society is exposing me far more indecently and violating my private life. Yet it was indecent, that encounter. I was admittedly mad with grief, and wanted to destroy myself, and had not Miss Koch arrived when she did I might have done so in an act of atonement for the death of Labby. But it was the infidelity to my dead love that was indecent. In this also I am guilty.

I have read through what I have written, and recognize that to have tried myself is no defence. I accept my guilt, and can pronounce my sentence, even death, but this all takes place inside my own head. In the Courtroom, in the presence of people who know nothing, and I believe can know nothing of the workings of my mind, anything that happens can only be a clumsy parody of my own judgement. Then why does this confrontation across the space of a Public Courtroom with a so-called judge so terrify me, a petty Solomon to whom I am merely a disagreeable impediment between him and the first whisky and soda of the day?

If only I could plead guilty and accept my punishment by letter, or even telephone. Why does the system require that I should stand there in person? Convicts don't labour in public. Eric tells me I can expect nine months at most. If it is like this it will not be disagreeable. But I would rather serve thirty years' hard labour than walk into that room tomorrow morning. I close my eyes and imagine a court with cream radiators, the smell of disinfectant, one heavy, scuffed leather chair, and a gallery ringing the room like a bear-pit. Excited red faces, come to see the freak: Bee's predatory red mouth, Nat's awful nose and strip-club leer, Mrs Peacock, Bob Makins, Mr Smart, Miss Koch and Mummy. All waiting to hear what I think about before I go to sleep. The thought terrifies me.

I am disturbed by another image, a memory of childhood

that ambushes me at every turn of thought. I was seven, and Dad had just come to collect me from hospital where Mummy had sent me for tests because she thought I had TB. The doctor told Dad that there was nothing wrong with my lungs, and we left. I felt a great joy at being out of the hospital, sitting on the mailbags in the back of Dad's van, driving down an avenue of tall trees that were very pale green in the bright sunlight. The sun was in my eyes, and each tree passed between me and the sun as if they were gliding by between us. Dad wanted to stay out for a bit, and stopped his van in a little park the other side of Mundham where there used to be a pond. There was a horse-chestnut beside the pond, and as I reached the first cleft I was so giddy with happiness that I had to cling on to the smooth round bough to stop myself falling. The heavy mysterious scent of the flower-candles, the cleaner smell of the leaves and the massy strength of the fork seemed suddenly safer than anything I had ever known. I clung and clung, till my legs and arms were stiff and I heard Dad calling me down below through the green palmate leaves.

How can I entertain such erotic thoughts? Much against my will my manhood rose twice today, until my intense shame cowed its arrogance. There can be no tree after Labby. How can I bear the next thirty years, struggling with this upstart devil in the flesh, this wrinkled, brooding Mephistopheles? Brian has brought me a sleeping pill. I am going to take it.

EXCERPT FROM THE INTIMATE JOURNAL OF ROSE HOPKINS

I have got to go to Reading after all. The policewoman told me what to say and I am going to wear my Junior gym slip and suspenders. What will be best of all will be the ride in the car. Mummy and Daddy and Auntie Emily are going in their car, and I shall be ALONE with Charlie. Miss

Brownlow says I have the most beautiful eyes in the world. We went to Windsor in the bus and she had her hand on my knee all the way. The orchestra was super. Mr Barenbum was HUGE, but Miss Brownlow said she liked the girl who played the cello. I told Miss Brownlow I would like to see his, and she said she would show me her rolling pin. Coming home in the bus she bit my ear and it bled. The conductor thought she was my father, and we all had a giggle. Mum and Dad were waiting for me at the bus-stop and Miss Brownlow was livid. At school today she followed me into the lavs.

LETTER FROM MESSRS GWATKIN, CAZENOVE AND HITLER TO MR CHAS SMART

Dear Charles,

I've just had a letter from Len Strangeways. It's always awkward when I find two clients, both old friends, getting across one another and there is a real possibility of legal proceedings being initiated.

May I speak to you Charles, man to man. Couldn't you give up this diarrhoea business? It can't be getting you anywhere, and people are beginning to talk. Image-wise it's a non-starter.

This has been a trying carry-on for us all, but now that the police have got the Borer, why shouldn't we all bury the hatchet? Madge and I are giving a little wine and cheese do tomorrow night about seven, and Len said he might drop by. It's wonderful what a glass or two of Len's Burgundy can do to break the ice.

Yours,

Sid. (Gwatkin)

LETTER FROM MISS KOCH TO MRS BEATRICE GROSS

Dear Mrs Gross!

Mrs Mackevoy has asked me that I should write to you to thank you for your letter. She is very well but is in her bedroom at the moment throwing a medicine ball about.

First she asks me to say 'Hello' to your Dobermann, second to say that Humphrey is at present in the Reading police station, awaiting trial for something which he has not done. She thanks you for your offer of help and asks only for your discretion. The trial is tomorrow (Mum is the Word) at 10.30 in the Reading Magistrates' Court. He has asked that no one should go there, and hopefully he will be back in Mundham tomorrow night. Please, not a word.

Mrs Mackevoy sends her Greetings,

U. Koch.

LETTER FROM THE MUNDHAM SANITARY INSPECTOR TO
ALDERMAN STRANGEWAYS

Dear Len,

As you know we've had cause to speak our minds to each other in the past about the constituents of your Low-Calorie Wine. I've now had a tip-off to the effect that you are going beyond the limits of adulteration we came to terms on.

Crude chemicals, vegetable waste, slaughter-house effluent and an acceptable level of pigeon-droppings I am prepared to go in to bat for, but when it comes to human ordure I refuse to stick my neck out.

Please see that this practice stops or you may find a less sympathetic person in my successor.

Yours faithfully,

E. F. Wilcox.

JOHN FORTUNE & JOHN WELLS

EXCERPT FROM THE *Mundham Advertiser*

Mundham Man on Sex Charge

Reading Court Sensation

A Mundham man was sent to prison
for three months today by a Reading
Magistrate. He is Humphrey
Mackevoy, 41, of 32, Albuhera Drive,
Mundham, proprietor of Glock and
Sons, Booksellers. Mackevoy pleaded
guilty to two charges of inflicting
malicious damage on Council
Property, and of indecently exposing
himself. A charge of assaulting a 15-
year-old schoolgirl was dismissed.
Passing sentence on Mackevoy, the
Magistrate, Sir Hector Bredalbane QC
said that this was one of the most
unusual cases to have come before
him in twenty-five years on the Bench.
He accepted that the accused was an
intelligent man, and that he had acted
under sexual compulsion: but as yet
sexual compulsion was no offence in
the law. Mackevoy asked for 409 other
offences to be taken into
consideration.

Laughter in Court

Pale and neatly dressed in a brownish
tweed suit, Mackevoy listened
impassively as Inspector Herbison for
the prosecution recounted the
circumstances of his arrest. There was
laughter in the public gallery as the

Inspector told how, on the night of November 5th, police surprised Mackevoy in Paradise Woods, Mundham, in the act of sexual intercourse with a tree, the property of Mundham Rural District Council. Asked amid near-uproar how such a thing was possible, Inspector Herbison placed in evidence a brace and bit, found at the scene of the offence. At this point a member of the public shouted a comment which caused renewed laughter in the gallery. The woman, who described herself as a housewife, Mrs Anne Peacock, 27, of Albuhera Drive, Mundham, was then asked to leave the Court. While this was going on Mackevoy was seen to sway in the dock, and wiped his lips with a handkerchief.

Intercourse

A 16-year-old schoolgirl then gave her evidence. Speaking in a clear, confident voice, the girl, who was dressed in a long black coat, alleged that on the night of the 5th she had been accosted by Mackevoy who had exposed himself to her and used obscene language. Under cross-examination by the accused, who conducted his own defence, the girl admitted to having had sexual intercourse with at least twenty men, some of whom were prominent in the world of entertainment. The Magistrate then ruled that this charge be dismissed and called for the police psychiatrist's report.

A Normal Life

Before passing sentence, Sir Hector asked the accused whether he had anything to say. Mackevoy, gripping the rail and speaking with obvious emotion, asked to be sent to prison for life. Amid more laughter Sir Hector regretted that he could not comply with the defendant's request. 'By your compulsive self-indulgence,' Sir Hector went on, 'you have put a great many people to a great deal of needless worry and expense. Your action in joining the Tree Defence League smacks, to say the least of it, of hypocrisy, and in giving you a light sentence I am taking into account the fact that you have already suffered a good deal and may still, on your release from prison, be encouraged to take up a normal life. You will go to prison for three months.' Mackevoy showed no signs of emotion as he heard the sentence, thanked the Magistrate, and was led from the Court to a waiting police car. A small crowd jeered as he was driven away.

Dear Sir/Madam,

Following certain complaints from postmen with regard
to the state of your porch and letterbox, I regret to inform
you that this Office is suspending further deliveries under
Section B6105 of the Post Office and Telecommunications
Act of 1959. When the nuisance has been dealt with you
may apply to this Office for a resumption of deliveries
subject to a satisfactory report from a Post Office Inspector.

B. Vernon,

Postmaster.

My darling little Fluff-Fluff,

Thank you for your silly, darling note.* How sensitive
you are, how easily hurt! I don't even remember you
lighting your pipe while we were waiting for the porter to
take our little bag downstairs. I do agree that a 'good smack
on the bottom', as you call it, has its place, but lighting up
wasn't bad enough for that, was it? I love the smell of your
pipe! While you were in the bathroom I have to confess I
put it in my mouth. So you see, silly Fluff-Fluff, it's you
who should be smacking me!

How lovely it was lying side by side in that great big bed
watching the cars go past on the ceiling. It was heaven
playing with your moustache in the darkness. I wanted to
run my hand over your face all night, until I knew every
bump by heart. I think we're so right to take things

* Apparently lost. H.M.

109

gradually, and you were so sweet about keeping your trousers on. I know it was a silly thing to ask, but I do think we must talk over every step of the way along the primrose path to intimacy. And as you saw, I'm afraid, I shall get very cross if you try to rush things.

I'm so sorry I smacked your dear hand, but it wasn't hard, was it?

I thought all in all the trial might have been a lot worse. You looked divine in your uniform, and every time I looked at your trousers I blushed to think where they'd been the night before. I had a word with Sir Hector afterwards, and he said, quite rightly, that if it hadn't been for Humphrey there wouldn't have been any spraying. There is a leader in the Advertiser called ' This Evil Man ', fully justified in my view, and one silly cartoon,* but otherwise I think most people's sympathy is still with the T.D.L. I have his mother here at the moment – it seemed the only way of getting Ursie back – and she's in a very bad way, I'm afraid. She has an absolutely infuriating way of slamming the door of the bedside cabinet when she wants Ursie. Dr Phillips is in and out of the house like a tit at nesting time but he did tell me the most marvellous news about Smart. He's apparently got some awful germ in his stomach and Phillips thinks it's driving him mad. He says he's in agony, which has quite made my day.

I know you're desperately busy, but do come on Thursday, if only for a drink, and we can have a proper chat about Stage Two.

Love and kisses,

Buzzie.

---

* The cartoon showed myself in conversation with a woodpecker and the Caption ' If you knows of a better 'ole, go to it!' H.M.

EXCERPT FROM THE INTIMATE JOURNAL OF ROSE HOPKINS

What can I do? Dad and Mum are livid. I have been locked in my room for telling fibs at Reading, and I have got a black eye where Dad hit me. I look awful. I hate H.M. I would like to put his thing through a mincer. He is so mean. How could I have loved him? I have rubbed his name off my hairbrush. Why does it always happen to me? I feel like an old woman and yet I am only sixteen. Barry came round tonight but Mum wouldn't let him in, so he hung about in the garden. In the end I opened the window. He has had all his hair cut off and looks fab. He said he had got some Durex but Dad heard him and chased him up the road.

EXCERPT FROM THE DIARY OF HUMPHREY MACKEVOY*

My first day in prison. My uniform, though well-laundered, is rough and chafes me under the arms and between the legs. As this is an open prison I have my own room in which I am now sitting. The door is not locked and anyone, I suppose, could come in at any time. I feel not so much an aversion to society as a sharp desire for solitude. I started work today in the prison library as assistant to a man who strangled his wife. It is a pitiful collection of books, principally theology and Westerns, and even one theological Western written by the prison chaplain, the Reverend Percy Luff. I have not met him yet, but I am told he is 'a card'.

The prison consists of eight brick huts, workshops, a canteen, a sick bay, a guardroom and the library, which is a tar-papered hut with a wooden veranda. All the buildings date from the last war. On one side of the compound the ground plan of a very large church has been dug, and

---

* This and subsequent entries are written in a buff exercise book. H.M.

prisoners are asked to contribute voluntary labour. The buildings are surrounded by a high barbed-wire fence, screened by young maples. I would much have preferred to have been incarcerated in a prison of the sort I have seen in films: the galleries of iron doors, the clank of buckets and the clang of inspection traps, exercise in a bare concrete yard, bars, chimneys, high walls, and the only reminder of nature a scrofulous pigeon on the window-sill.

The only concession here to my aesthetic demands is the angled twelve-foot fence of barbed-wire, but even that is too near to the trees for my comfort. The reason I crave such a dungeon of concrete and iron, I know, is that I wish to be broken, to be saved from myself, from my own nature. I desperately want to live without torment. I have always been guided by my body, and it has brought me here, to the further shores of grief. I wanted to love Labby alone, but my body betrayed me. I knew with my reason that what I was doing was wrong and could only hurt Labby, but reason was never the master. In a word I cannot trust my body: if I am to devote myself to that true, pure love, it is necessary for me to be excluded from temptation.

As it is I must make my own prison. Last night, after lights out – I arrived at six with only time to be issued with my clothes and bedding – I began to build it in my mind. This is where I shall go when I am alone. I managed to concentrate fully on a completely blank white wall until I fell asleep.

No shadow of a branch fell across it, no rustle of leaves disturbed its chaste peace. I tried in a clumsy way to explain what I meant to the Governor this morning but it was hopeless. I dread to think I interest him: his eyes never left my face for the five minutes I was with him and I can hear him this evening discussing me with his wife in his well-meaning Hampstead clichés over their rug-making.

He terrified me with his easygoing expansiveness – he looks like T. S. Eliot – and humiliated me as I was leaving by saying with a chuckle that the trees in the compound were 'for looking at'. I was near to despair. What I wanted was the staring malevolence of a Kitchener, a gaoler who could lock up my mind and prove to me that nature was dead.

He is like Bredalbane. When I walked into the Court I expected a judge who would denounce me without caring who I was or how I felt. A remote headmaster, who would deliver a well-worn moral lecture, impersonal and unassailable. Instead I found myself looking at a man as weak as I was, obscenely naked of authority, trying to be friendly. I have remembered it all a hundred times since yesterday. It was more humiliating than my worst fears had led me to expect. Stoneley, the policeman I had met at Bars, offered me a cigarette before we went in and talked about Miss Longridge. He also unnerved me by his ingratiating manner.

The first thing I noticed when I went in was the gallery, almost exactly as I had imagined it, the hostile faces of the Grosses in the front row, Bee with her opera glasses, Mrs Peacock in a ludicrous feathered hat, Miss Koch trying not to weep. I did not recognize Mummy at first. But the audience was the only element of drama. Otherwise the atmosphere, then and throughout the encounter, was like being in a post office.

As the circumstances of my arrest were described by an Inspector I had not seen before with a bald head and thick glasses, the laughter began. It was not so much its effect on me as its inappropriateness. I felt far away and dazed as I glanced up at the spectacle of red-rimmed mouths gobbling air, gold fillings and lolling tongues. I felt embarrassed for them, and wished they could behave. When Mrs Peacock shouted 'Oak for a poke, eh?' I felt only contempt for her vulgarity and relief when she was hustled out.

Then came the charade with the flabby Mata Hari. According to her well-rehearsed fantasy, accompanied by what she no doubt thought of as seductive mannerisms, I had been obsessed with her beauty for some weeks, had followed her everywhere, and had watched her undressing through a pair of German field glasses. On Wednesday night I had jumped out of the bushes, shouted 'I love you, I love you, I love you, what about a spot of muff-diving?' – whatever that may be – and torn her skirt over her head. It was fortunate for me that the girl possessed so little charm, otherwise I might have had difficulty in refuting what she said. When I put it to her that she hardly seemed the kind of girl that a man would find irresistible, she denied it fiercely, and claimed that she had had sexual intercourse with at least twenty men, including such diverse figures as 'Bobby Charlton, David Frost, Georgie Fame, Lord Mountbatten' and 'a bishop'. I had no need to interrupt her tirade. When she had finished, my liberal friend on the bench dismissed her and discussed her for some moments with a Probation Officer. As the crush of Hogarth faces leered down from the gallery I shrank back into myself, fixing my mind on Labby's severed stump, and forcing myself to gaze on the marks of the saw. What was my grief compared with this? Labby with me, transfigured in her golden chains and I was beyond pain or distraction.

I must do something about these trousers. They emphasize every tiny movement, inflaming the most transient glow to a potential furnace. I am very far now from the peace I felt in the dock. I must build, build, for the forest can so easily break in. I am writing this on my lap and already the page is beginning to buckle. I must stop writing and think *concrete thoughts*.

LETTER FROM MISS KOCH TO HUMPHREY MACKEVOY

My dear Humphrey!

Only three months! I have spoken with Inspector Reggie, a kind good man, about your place of captivity, and he has told me it is very modern and humane. How wonderful! Already at the end of this month I will come to visit you with your Mama, if she is well again.

As you see I am back in the Nest where Miss Longridge needs me. She is so happy that I am returned and gay and sings to herself all day. Oh Humphrey! I wish you could see her. The weather today was so beautiful, we have made a great walk together. As we have returned back this evening I remembered the poem of our Goethe :

> ' Over all peaks
> Is peace
> In all tree-tops
> You feel
> Barely a breath
> The little birds are silent in the wood
> Wait only
> Soon
> You will also be at peace. '

Forgive the translation, I have been unable to show the rhymes, but it is done with love. Your mother was sick on the eiderdown today, but we forgive her always. Oh Humphrey, when she has heard you say that you are guilty and that you must go to prison it was as if the life has gone out from her. Do not worry yourself, I am sure she will be well again. She was so strong and full of fun! Now she lies all day on her bed and reads the poems of Worcester. My, how she can bang, that woman! But we love her. All day it is Ursie come here this minute, Ursie where are my pills,

Ursie call the doctor I am dying damn you, up and down the stairs, up and down, up and down. How I love her sense of humour. I speak to her so much of you, Humphrey, I ask how you were as a small child, and I talk of how it will be when we are together, and who knows, perhaps with little ones! She does not say anything, but I can tell from her expression she is thinking of you. Today Mrs Peacock is arrived with Frobisher more dead than alive. But Ethne has given him vodka and he has run about like a puppy and fallen asleep in the coalbucket. What a sweet old dog he is! We call him Stink-Cheese. This afternoon the Ornithological Society is meeting again, and tonight Inspector Reggie is coming and we are making a glow-wine. We will drink it to your health, dear Humphrey,

Prost! and many dear Greetings,

Your Ursula.

LETTER FROM MRS GROSS TO MRS F. MACKEVOY

Dear Mrs Mackevoy,

I thought you'd like to know that what that filthy Humphrey of yours has done has made me so ill I've had to go to bed. How could he do anything so swinish? When I think I've had you both in my house, fed you my food and my drink and all the time that twisted pervert was messing about with my trees I just want to vomit.

Bee has just been sick and I sympathize with her.* Your room still smells of piss and if you as much as show your face round here again I'll punch it. There's no place near decent people for swines like you.

B. and N. Gross.

* This paragraph is in Nat's unsteady handwriting. H.M.

116

Bernard Armitage, the murderer and chief librarian, has gone to see the psychiatrist and I am in charge of the library. No one has been in all the morning, and I am painfully becoming conscious, as after an anaesthetic, of the difference between my life now in this hut full of grubby books and my life, only a few days ago, in my poor burned shop. I am sitting at an old Army table with an oil stove beside me. Its smell has permeated all the books, and those on my table – two Zane Greys and *For Christ's Sake* by the Bishop of Woolwich – are greasy and falling apart. Someone has blown his nose into *Gunfight Canyon*, and I cannot separate the pages.

I have been trying to read the chaplain's *Posse from Galilee*. The book deals with the activities of a band of twelve Jewish Immigrants, headed by their leader Sheriff Jesus, and is set in the Wild West in the 1870s. The plot is based fairly closely on the Gospel narrative, and after a miraculous clambake at which Jesus is elected Sheriff of Sin City, they roam the desert rescuing wagons from marauding Indians and restoring the victims to life. Later in the book Sheriff Jesus preaches the Sermon on Boot Hill and washes the feet of Calamity Magdalene at the Arimathea Saloon. During a game of twelve-handed poker Wild Judas Iscariot, one of the Posse, is accused of cheating and subsequently betrays the Sheriff to a gang of rustlers led by Caiphus the Kid in cahoots with the Chicago Railroad Baron Pontius Pilate III. The Sheriff is ambushed in Calvary Gulch and badly shot up. After lying all day in the hot sun he expires and is buried in a garden at the back of the Arimathea Saloon. The Posse takes to the hills. Three days later Calamity Magdalene is shooting at cans in the garden when she is approached by someone she does not at first recognize. It is, of course, the Risen Sheriff. At this point the book departs from the Bible Story, presumably out of deference to progressive theology, and they get married and go back to Palestine, whence their return is dreaded by the hard-drinking rustlers and badmen of the plains. It is an appalling book. I contemplate my first meeting with its author with feelings of acute embarrassment.

In the shop now I would be warming the brown teapot while the electric kettle bubbled, surrounded by a private order of my own creating. From the set of Yorick's Sermons in the little bookcase on my desk to the faded letter from Thoreau to Emerson on the publication of Walden Pond that was framed above it, all burned. And replaced by this caricature. On the wall opposite me is a large calendar showing for the month of November a woman with enlarged breasts and red-painted lips powdering her behind with a pink powder-puff. Someone has drawn a disembodied penis in biro with the outline of a pair of testicles attached pointing towards the woman's rectum. Beneath it, brought in a few moments ago by a man with a crew-cut and dark glasses, is a thumbed paperback called Billy Graham on Golf.

I did not sleep well last night. I think I was kept awake by the sound of men in other rooms shouting in their sleep. I lay on my back, holding my eyes tight shut and desperately trying to create slab by slab my concrete fortress. As I began building I forced myself to look only at the first course of concrete slabs lying in a rough circle around me, dimly aware beyond them of the still uncreated elements of my prison - the sound of a key turning in a lock, a door slamming, the perspective of a high wall and watchtowers. The walls of my cell grew higher, and I built a window with bars and a view of another brick wall beyond.

It was only when I looked up, full of confidence that I

would only see the pale grey sky and hear the wind, that I saw their rustling tops. Birnam Wood was on the march again. They grew higher and bent to shake their leaves at me. They were aspens, *populus tremula*. I shrank into a corner and felt their little round marginally-toothed leaves brush against my bare shoulders. Even as I turned my face from them I could see the sweet crotches of grey-barked soft white wood and felt my manhood hard as iron. I forced myself to build a ceiling, but even as it found its way into place above me I knew the aspens' long searching roots were beneath me, forcing themselves against my crouching buttocks.

I switched on the light, threw back the bedclothes, and summoning all my resolve I stared at my arrogant manhood with contempt. Slowly it wilted, and to make doubly sure I emptied my tooth glass over it. I turned out the light again and tried to think of Labby as I had done in the dock, glorious in flower against a blue heaven, no longer in the earth but whole and alone and floating, blazing like the sun in the sky. Peace flooded into my mind, and I realized that with this vision before me I was unassailable and did not need my fortress: but that when it faded I would have to build the fortress again, and this time more secure. I think I must have fallen asleep then, because when I was woken by the bell at seven-thirty I was concerned only with the mundane irritations of getting up on a cold morning.

12.30 I had to break off there as the Chaplain came in. He has the wettest palms I have ever encountered. He is younger than myself, short, slightly-built and with an unusually wide clerical collar that causes him to hold his chin permanently in the air and gives him a supercilious expression. He has a habit of saying 'Yes, yes', over and over again to himself in the pauses in the conversation created by his own shyness, and in this case mine. He told me, to my relief, that he was not going to ask me why I was here, and that he was probably as great a sinner as I was, probably greater. ('Yes, yes.') He asked me whether I had asked Jesus to come into my heart and I had to confess that I had not. He then saw that I had been reading his book and brightened. It was, he said, a very simple way of telling the old, old story for simple people in simple terms, and he asked me whether I liked it. I managed to mutter something vaguely complimentary, which I immediately regretted, as I have now agreed to read the proofs of his latest book, *Jesus and the Red Planet*, which he tells me is based on the same plot. I also said I would attend what he calls his little service in the canteen on Sunday mornings when I can.

I feel an urgent need for some more demanding discipline, if only to keep my mind occupied. I have never thought much about religion, partly I suppose because of the example of Daddy's quiet profession of Buddhism, and also because of Mummy's determination to have me ordained. But I am now intrigued by the possibility of something more austere than the Chaplain's embarrassing platitudes. In the last few days phrases from the New Testament have come back to me: 'If thine eye offend thee, pluck it out,' in particular. It is not the theology of Christianity that attracts me but the discipline of mysticism, the rigours of its moral gymnasium. I am determined to make myself what I devoutly wish to be.

MINUTES OF A MEETING OF THE MUNDHAM
ORNITHOLOGICAL SOCIETY

Opening the meeting, the President, Miss Ethne Longridge, OM, DSO and Bar, regretted that there were signs of backsliding among members. Attendance had been poor and subscriptions were only coming in slowly. She herself had been the only member of the Society to have attended a Dawn Watch-In on November 7th at Priory Pond to observe a pair of phalarope. She therefore proposed to fine all members of the Society 7/6d to be earmarked for the Hospitality Fund. At this point there were interruptions and Miss Longridge was urged to make a statement about the position of Mr Humphrey Mackevoy, Honorary Secretary of the Tree Defence League.

Miss Longridge replied that Mr Mackevoy, for whom she had never entertained any respect, had flouted the laws of Nature and was now paying the penalty. His greatest crime was that he had clouded the issue of the Fringed Woodpecker. There was no doubt in her mind, she said, that in every case it was the bird that had done the spade-work, and that Mackevoy had merely put the creature's patient excavation to a disgraceful use. This would also, she was convinced, be the considered opinion of the Royal Ornithological Society when the relevant evidence was laid before them. The President was supported in this by Miss Ursula Koch, who said that she had discovered a number of holes in the vicinity of the reservoir which could not possibly have been put to human use.

Despite appeals from the Chair for calm, Mrs Townsend, formerly of the Sightings Committee, rose to her feet and made an emotional speech in which she demanded that the President step down. Her motion that 'Anybody who couldn't spot a common or garden bare-faced sex-maniac when they saw one had no place among decent bird-watchers', and that 'the President should resign immediately', was carried by four votes to two. Miss Longridge, in tendering her resignation, wished it to be written into the minutes that she was resigning from the Presidency under pressure from a group of ingrate alcoholics. The meeting came to an end amid noisy scenes.

LETTER FROM THE GOVERNOR OF DROXFORD OPEN PRISON TO
GRAHAM NIPPLE ESQUIRE FRCS

Dear Nipple,

Thank you for your letter and the report on Mackevoy.
He seems a nice enough chap, but, as you say, plum loco.

I'm sure you're absolutely right about the Aversion
Therapy, though I must say it was extraordinary what a few
volts in the right place did to Stan MacIntosh, our
pickpocket. So much so that every time he wants to blow his
nose he's sick. I'm not suggesting this is an ideal situation,
but should he take to crime again he will be a good deal
easier to trace.

Perhaps after all it might be worth bringing your bag of
tricks down for Mackevoy. Anyway, let me know what you
think and I'll get him to sign a form.

Barbara's penis envy is much better now she's got one of
her own.

Yours ever,

Mike.

EXCERPT FROM THE DIARY OF HUMPHREY MACKEVOY

Will it never go down? Everywhere I look there is wood.
The table, the bed, the chair. All victims, like Labby. And
not just wood! In every machined limb I read a name -
sycamore, oak, white pine, *pinus strobus* - and see it as it was,
trembling in the sunlight. I pity them, I know I am guilty of
their destruction, but I want them all the more. Even this
paper, furrowed and rucked up by the nib of my pen, nags
me with the image of the pine that was felled, rolled in
rivers, cut and macerated into pulp to make it. And my guilt
forces me to stand by the lumberjack and watch his shining
axe as it thuds into the sweet resiny trunk. Oh God!

EXCERPT FROM THE MUNDHAM ADVERTISER

Mystery Bug Hits Mundham

*Local Doctors 'Swept Off
Their Feet'*

Mundham's doctors are having their busiest time since the Mao Flu Epidemic of last winter. Hundreds of local residents have fallen victims to the new mystery virus that has swept doctors off their feet with a flood of telephone calls and urgent requests for treatment. Mundham Cottage Hospital is on Red Alert, and although hospital staff are confident that the situation is under control, the Matron, Miss Eartha Hargreaves said 'we are treating this as an emergency'.

Gippy Tummy

The symptoms include 'gippy tummy', fainting fits, pains in the back and sickness. The Chief Medical Officer of Health for Mundham, Dr E. G. Phillips is investigating the possibility of food poisoning being the cause. Mundham's last epidemic of this kind was the so-called 'Doughnut Affair' of 1953, when hundreds of Mundham schoolchildren were taken ill after eating tainted confectionery.

EXCERPT FROM THE DIARY OF HUMPHREY MACKEVOY

I am exhausted. For a week my organ has been like a Jack-in-the-Box. I achieve perhaps a few minutes of peace and then the lid flies off and there it is again: a signal for sexual fantasies to crowd into my mind, and break down the walls of my resolve. It is worse at night. I have never touched myself. Even at school, where it seemed the fashion, and yet the desire grows more complex and irresistible with every day I spend in prison, mocking my best efforts. Each time I build my fortress it is more solid, a vast labyrinth in the mind, a Spandau in which I am the Hess: each time I meditate on Labby I feel closer to its essence, its purity, its true Nature. I have discovered the relationship between love and sacrifice and suffering, which, if I can only conquer these overwhelmingly lewd promptings, might preserve and sustain me for the rest of my life. Even as I write this I can feel my trousers stretch and lift, and I am in the spring wood at the bottom of Church Meadow. . . Very well then, damned intruders welcome! I will write them down, and doing so, exorcize them.

I am thinking now, as I have so often this week, of my first Experience, when I lost my virginity. It was Ascension Day, a whole holiday from school at the end of April, and I had just had my fourteenth birthday. The weather was more like June and I had spent the morning in the nets trying to develop a leg-break. I remember going back to the changing room out of the singing sunlight and the smell of vests and socks and stale sweat and the cricket-pads lying on the floor. I changed into khaki shorts and a blue shirt and sandals, went into the unventilated, fly-buzzing classroom for my copy of *The Prelude*, bought a cheese roll at the Tuck Shop and put them in my saddle-bag.

Free-wheeling through the leafy lanes I saw the greenness for the first time that year: the month had been wet and we had been cooped up indoors a great deal. I listened to the ticking of my milometer as I turned downhill into a wooded valley with a river running through it. In the village I locked my bicycle against the churchyard wall and taking my book from the saddle-bag, walked down across the empty meadow to the wood by the river, eating my cheese roll.

The place was old. Moss had spread between the bulging, twisted trunks of oak and ash and hornbeam, and the sunlight through the leaves lit patches of daffodils. Everything seemed enamelled: primroses, aconites and wood anemones, campions and clumps of foxglove, and all under some indefinable enchantment. The birds had stopped singing as I sat down with my back against a fallen tree, green with moss, and now, all at once they began singing again. A blackbird I remember, and a wood-pigeon.

I opened my book, but Wordsworth failed to hold my attention. His was a Nature of mighty presences, brooding peaks, the lake reflecting the sky, but I was among intimacy. I found myself stroking the soft cushions of moss, and watched a bumble-bee tumbling in the bell of a foxglove. I took off my shirt and opened my shorts. As I did so I saw my penis uncurl, fill and stiffen, as if summoned to some conspiracy with the wood. It swayed as if dancing to the birdsong. I stood up and my shorts slipped off. I took off my pants, marvelling at the stiff recoil of my member, and began to walk warily about, barefoot among the flowers, its pink head swaying in front of me. On impulse I knelt before a foxglove, and trembling, guided my member into the flower-cup. I felt an insect-flurry and looking down saw the humblest of bumble-bees crawl over the petal-lip, leaving me to my delicate exploration. The flower opened, and I experienced a shudder of mystery and desire.

Withdrawing I kissed the downy purple and then saw

that the dome of my penis was flecked with golden dust. I stood again, and was panting as I sauntered open-handed across the clearing. One dead trunk was entwined with convolvulus. I explored one white trumpet with my tongue, and then placed it delicately on my penis. A party hat! I was proud that I could wear it as I walked without it falling off. I imagined a stamen piercing that secret mouth. I tore at primroses and rubbed them over my belly. Just then I saw an oak that I realize now to have been diseased. In the bole, surrounded by a halter of swollen wood, was a dark declivity, seeping brown moisture. I was clumsy, but Nature was with me, and as the clearing buckled silently, I felt a pain behind my eyes and fell against the ribbed bark, clinging there for support.

I was ashamed then, certainly. But as I put on my clothes in a panic that I had been seen or would be discovered, I was aware of the wood echoing the satisfaction that I also felt. I remember resting on my handlebars at the top of the hill and looking back across the deserted valley at the dense tops of those trees, now no larger in the heat than a tuft of grass, and wanting to laugh with happiness. For better or for worse I was now a man. And still am.

So, I am still erect. Five minutes to lights out. It should be easy, at this time of year, to spread concrete over the dead earth when the sun is in the remote North, to put an axe through the dormant roots, to build an exercise yard for the mind with a high wall against my memories. In writing them down I have tried to make a garden. But while the order is mine, it is an imaginary one. The roots can crack paving stones. I can never say it is dead.

EXCERPT FROM THE INTIMATE JOURNAL OF ROSE HOPKINS

I am in love with Barry! Last night he came round late with his Dad's ladder and climbed up to my bedroom window. I was wearing my orange see-through nightie with the frills, sitting up in bed with my 'Vampire Mag'. My blood ran cold when I heard him knocking at the window. Then I heard him call my name and I rushed to meet him. I opened the window and he could look right down my cleavage. I tried to pull him in, but he was scared, and grazed his tummy on the iron thing that sticks up on the window ledge, so he stayed standing on the ladder. We kissed and he put his tongue in my mouth. It was bliss. Then he made me take my nightie off, and I did!

I said I would not let him come through the window until he had put his Durex on. He got it out, but I could not see it in the dark. Drat! Then he dropped the Durex in the bushes and had to climb down to get it. It took him a long time and I heard Dad going to the toilet again. When Barry came back up the ladder he said he had it on and I let him kiss me again through the window and put my tongue in his mouth. Heaven! But then he got his cramps and slid down the ladder. It made such a 'racket' that Dad started swearing and then came out of the toilet. He came into my room and I pretended it was the window-cleaner but Dad did not believe me and saw Barry lying on the grass with his knees all bent up. Dad shouted some horrible things and Mum came in furious and said the neighbours were knocking on the wall. Dad was really screaming, and ran downstairs to get Barry, but Barry pulled the ladder away and ran off. Dad says he's smashed his cucumber frames. Good job too! I hate him! They have taken away all my frilly undies but I don't care. It was worth it. I love Barry. He is so brave. And his mouth tastes much better than Miss Brownlow's.

EXCERPT FROM THE DIARY OF HUMPHREY MACKEVOY

Mummy arrived this morning, having driven overnight in an electric invalid chair without any kind of lights. She had been in the ditch twice, and had lost her wig. Mr Voyce came to collect me from the library and I found her sitting alone in the interview room dressed entirely in black, streaked with dried mud, and noisily drinking a mug of tea. The hair had begun to grow again and her head was covered with a fine down of grey hair that looked like mould on a ball of blue Stilton. Mummy did not say anything, and neither did I. I sat opposite her on a stool. She could have been weeping, or suffering from a heavy cold or watching television: in either case the rhythmic sniffing was the same.

I realized how much I had put her out of my mind since the trial, how selfish I had been, and suddenly felt a great affection for Mummy. I suppose I had thought, kneeling in front of her in the Police Station in Reading, that I had somehow received absolution, and had no more obligation towards her. She finished her tea, and belched. I buried my head in my hands. When I looked up, she too had laid her head on the table, and was banging it softly against the wood with a series of muffled thuds.

I told her that I had changed, that I would never look at another tree, that I would get married and that she could come and live with us, that we would have babies to delight her old age.

She said that she did not like babies, and then banged her head so violently against the table that I feared she would break it. Of course she wanted me to get married, and why shouldn't I have children: her remark had been typical of her selfishness. The prospect of Mummy without her indomitable self-centredness was unbearable. I knew that I must interrupt her pitiful apology, which, once it got a hold, would be carried to extremes like everything she did. I asked her about the shop, and was pleased to see a gleam of indignation in her eye. She told me that an Insurance Investigator had been to see her at the Nest and told her that they were treating the fire as suspected arson: a charred drum of Spinelli's 'Fethoblast' had been found in the ashes.

Involuntarily I shouted 'Smart!' at which Mummy leapt up from the table, her eye blazing. She had not realized the connection. I told her of the warning, of the telephone call, and as I explained she paced around the room like a tiger. Her anger was infectious. I began to think of all the books, the rare editions that I had patiently collected all these years, the irreplaceable beauty of the bindings, the wisdom, instruction and delight contained in them. Mother agreed. To her there was no greater sacrilege than burning a book, and citing the Library at Alexandria, the martyrdom of Jan Hus and the Nazi bonfires, she began pounding the table, denouncing the Philistine, the Barbarian, Smart the Hun. Her shouts of 'I'll kill him' brought Mr Voyce running in, and as we sat on her to calm her, she cursed Smart for every mishap that had befallen us.

When she had recovered herself, she began to lay her plans. Mundham had been visited by a plague. Shortly after a drinks party which she had refused to attend because of the presence of Inspector Stoneley, Miss Koch, Miss Longridge and the Inspector had been convulsed with vomiting and diarrhoea. Mummy would take advantage of the desolation to work her havoc on Mr Smart. Miss Longridge had been unseated, after sixty-four years, from the Presidency of the Bird Club and suspected a plot. Mummy would avenge this insult too – Smart was at the bottom of it, she would be bound. I casually remarked that I had had a letter which identified Smart as Himmler – a foolish mistake as she believed it immediately. Now the deaths of millions of Jews were added to his crimes. Leaving the building she picked up her invalid carriage and threw it across the compound where it fell into one of the trenches forming the foundations of the church. Thereupon she hitched up her skirts over her knees, and ran off down the road raising a cloud of dust.

I turned to an astonished Mr Voyce, and requested permission to send her a telegram: 'For God's Sake do Nothing Foolish. Let our watchword be Stealth.'

I went to Mr Luff's service yesterday morning in the canteen. The place reeked of boiled cabbage. A tea-trolley with a cloth over it served as the altar and apart from the Strangler the only person there was a silent man with a square head who is said to have stolen a Hockney from the National Portrait Gallery. The words of the Liturgy were almost inaudible against the singing and laughter of the white-turbaned women preparing lunch, the rattling of crockery and the manhandling of large metal bins on the concrete floor. We sang one hymn, 'The Church's One Foundation', and Mr Luff preached a sermon on the text 'Consider the lilies of the field'.

As far as I could hear above the din, he was making an elaborate parallel between a lily and a radio telescope, the latter contemplating the Universe in search of Truth, rather than indulging in the active life of crime. At one point a chip was thrown from the kitchen, which fell in the Chalice. After a moment's hesitation, Luff took it out and held it in the candle flame where it sizzled and smoked for some time, eventually burning his fingers. One of the women must have been an astonishing marksman, for a moment later a raw lamb chop followed the chip into the Chalice, displacing most of the wine which splashed over and soiled the white tablecloth. This was too much for Luff, and the service was adjourned while he went to complain to the Governor.

During this interval I fell to idly turning the pages of my hymnbook. Someone had left a bookmarker among the hymns for Good Friday, a painted card with a red tassel and the words at the bottom in very small print: 'Vanheems' for all your liturgical needs.' Above this was a picture of St Francis, kneeling and looking up at crucifixion set in a golden aureole with the caption 'Calvary's Tree'.

I looked at the cross as I had never looked at it before. I understood for the first time, I think, the meaning of what is called the Divine Sacrifice, and in St Francis's expression I could recognize my own. In those blessed moments when Labby appears before me, transfigured in her glory, I am also transfixed by the suffering, the marks of the saw in the wood, the awful beauty of its symmetry in death. The Laburnum was always a victim: its seed was placed in that shabby corner of the garden by man, to grow as a decoration, to be used as cricket stumps, a target for knife-throwing, a urinal for dogs and cats, a surface for men to carve their names on and brand it with hearts pierced with arrows, and, not least, the willing victim of the violence of my body. And looking at the outspread arms of the cross, symbol of universal acceptance, I knew that it was willing: that the Tree, all trees, is the true image of selfless Nature.

My musings were interrupted by the return of Luff, who had not, it seemed, managed to find the Governor. By this time the altar had been wheeled away, the Strangler was asleep, the art-thief had gone into the kitchen to make eyes at one of the old women, and the vessels were being scoured. At first, Luff was a model of Christian patience. Shouting at the top of his voice, he called the kitchen staff into the canteen and then humbly apologized to them for losing his temper, explaining to them that there was nothing God liked better than a good joke. He then dismissed them and turned to his altar to continue. When he saw that it was no longer there, but stood in the corner, piled with soup plates, he went white with rage and tore his surplice off, flinging it on the ground and jumping on it. The lunch bell rang, and as the old women from the kitchen began shoving the chairs out of the rows in which they had been arranged for the service, the Chaplain picked up his white embroidered stole and flicked it at them until one old lady took it away from him and ran out through the kitchen with him in close pursuit.

I am still sleeping very badly. My nature-excluding imaginary citadel is now so large that I am beginning to feel terribly lonely. In every direction infinite corridors of cells stretch away: away through the concrete catacombs, overlaying and lying through each other: some have lights inside, but I have never seen another prisoner: I have heard warders in the corridors but I have never met them, and a penitential voice, that sometimes becomes the sound of a far-off power-saw or the confused murmur of traffic, drones improving sermons on the wickedness of Nature. It is no longer a conscious effort to imagine this place: I find myself there in dreams. In nightmares it becomes as insubstantial as projected light before the invasion of the forest. I wake up, writhing, often wet with sperm, seduced and unhappy. 'Oh what shall I do with this absurdity, that has been tied to me as to a dog's tail ?'* The simple truth is that neither the ascetic burden of the imaginary prison nor the guilty liberty of the erotic dreams can provide me with any real satisfaction or give any meaning to my life. Only love can do that, and Labby is gone. When I told Mummy that I would marry, I meant it. Perhaps with a wife, and constrained by the chains of responsibility and convention I could learn to turn my back on Nature and learn to love in a different way.

* From Yeats' poem, 'The Tower', 1928. H.M.

LETTER FROM INSPECTOR STONELEY TO MISS ETHNE
LONGRIDGE

Dearest Buzzie,

I am so ashamed at what happened the other night. I feel,
by your silence, that you do not want me to write to you, but
I must. I think I owe you some form of explanation.

The trouble started I think when Miss Koch refused to
realize when she wasn't wanted. I am as fond of yodelling as
the next man, but I wanted to be alone with you. I am afraid
I imbibed rather freely. When you finally sent her out to
count the owls I am afraid I was a bit unsteady on my pins
when it came to coming upstairs.

I know now what I said when we got into the bedroom
wasn't very well put (I blame the Vino), but what I meant to
say was that I am a very weak man. Every day I do things I
ought not to. You saw that night that despite our agreement
about Stage Two, I lost my head and interfered with your
blouse. Unless I have someone to correct me with a good
hard slapping, such as old Granny Whipmee used to
administer, I know I shall go from bad to worse. That's why
I insisted on six of the best, there and then. I fully realized
that you did not want to see my naked posterior - that would
have been absurd - but I think we'll find that things will
work out fine, once you've got the range, with you looking
the other way. Once and for all, you did not hit me too hard
with the walking-stick. I ran off like that on account of the
diarrhoea which was soon to engulf us all.

My trousers being down, I could not help tripping up
Ursula on the landing, not expecting to meet her, nor
realizing that she was bound for the same place. Please
convey my sincerest apologies to the lady in question.
Looking back, I realize that the worst thing I did, for which
I hope you'll severely punish me when next we meet, was
blocking up the sewage system with my trousers. I had had

a little accident en route and as I pulled the chain I merely held them in the little waterfall to give them a bit of a rinse. However I underestimated the force of the suction and the weight of the truncheon in the pocket, and was aghast to see them being dragged round the bend. That cistern certainly lives up to its name !

As I emerged from the toilet I instructed Miss Koch to avert her eyes, which she did, and it was then that I had the misfortune to slip and to fall against the china cabinet with such unhappy consequence. It was most good of you, after so much commotion, to agree to resume where we left off. What I cannot understand is why you couldn't have informed me that you were leaving the room when you did. Touching toes for ten minutes is no joke when nothing happens. After a bit I borrowed your bedspread and went to look for a taxi. I still cannot understand why you did it, Ethne. Was it to humiliate me? God knows, I deserve it. Let me have some word, if only a rude one. It's about time someone called me a pig or a rat or something.

I kiss your feet,

Your loving Fluff-Fluff.

EXCERPT FROM THE DIARY OF HUMPHREY MACKEVOY

I was talking to the Strangler this morning. He is really a very stupid man, and the only thing that has given his life any distinction is having killed his wife. He never stops talking about it, like a man who has won the Pools. He strangled her for laughing as he tried to make love to her. He tells me he has a woman in Droxford every Wednesday afternoon. She charges him four pounds. He describes things they do together that made me feel sick. He saw this, and defended himself by saying it was only natural. Fortunately he does not know what I am in prison for, so the

134

conversation ended there.

Thinking of my resolve to abandon trees for ever, I have been asking myself what it is about human beings that makes it impossible for me to love them. Even as a child I could not hear gushing demonstrations of affection, the pawings of aunts, and the determined way they tried to kiss my mouth always made me shrink. To say that I felt myself stifled against Mummy's woollen dresses is an understatement: the smell of all of them was like a foetid cupboard full of old clothes. It was the same at school. I used to get up at six in the summer and seven in winter to go to the showers, and the smell of the Maths Class after Gym is one of my clearest memories of those days. Mr Widdowson, who taught us Greek, had a habit of laying his hand on our necks when we were working, and I hated it. Any sort of physical contact, even in the rugger scrum, gave me the same feeling of wanting to escape.

It is not that I find all human beings ugly or disgusting. There was a boy at school who without question had the kind of body that Praxiteles might have sculpted: I have even believed myself in love, seeing a girl in a library lifting her hands to her hair. But these impressions are all fleeting, and only preserved in what we call works of art. Quite simply I cannot believe, and have never been able to believe, that Beauty is a human attribute. Perhaps I might fall in love with someone and find her utterly beautiful, but there would come a time when time itself, or a bad mood, a pimple or an illness would make her ugly: Beauty cannot survive in flesh, and I cannot love what is not beautiful.

How different it is with a tree. It grows instinctively in Beauty, containing in its seed the full form of its maturity. The tree is beautiful because it is what it is. It draws in its nourishment from the earth, its warmth from the sun, its moisture from the air, it reproduces itself without moving, letting its seed be carried on the wind. In all its myriad forms, from the fronded palm to the small-leaved elm and ash, it is the original paradigm of all living things: the Tree of Life. For man the need to move in order to eat and drink, the need to run after his life, to grow jointed limbs that enable him to do so, has banished him from the first possibility of Beauty. Man has fallen from the Tree. But even if a tree could move, even if by some metamorphosis it became a man, what a man it would be! Unquestioning, unselfish, undemanding, growing in symmetrical beauty into its death. Trees die standing up.*

I have been obsessed in the night hours with a particular tree, hardly a tree yet, a splendid slender sapling of a grey poplar that I had when I was nineteen. I had long since graduated to the drill, and those turbulent years were measured in the painful progression from $^3/_8''$ to $1^1/_4''$. I saw it from the window of a friend's car, driving back from a sale in a country house. It was early summer, and the poplar stood a little way back from the drive, naked by a waterfall, expressing in the fragile grace of its trunk such innocence, and in the delicacy of its upward-curving branches such helplessness that I became immediately erect. Back at College I somehow got through a tutorial on Smollett, and in the coolness of the evening while swallows swooped I mounted my bicycle and raced back, my drill clanking in my saddle-bag.

What thrills and tortures me even now is the savagery of the encounter. I flung my bicycle down in the bushes, undid my buttons, and released my straining rod, almost as thick, it seemed to me then, as the trunk I then attacked. I had to drill upwards, at an angle, for fear of penetrating it

* I had come across this line, 'Los arboles mueren de pie,' in Lorca I think. I later saw the flaw in this argument, as will be clear from subsequent entries.

completely. In our foreplay I tore off several branches and flung them to the winds. So, one after another, you helpless shrub, I'll tear down your defences. Hear that snap? It's going to be worse in a minute! Take this! Split! Yield! Lift! I felt the young roots tearing as I surged snorting into the gaping wood, upward and inward, fuck-fuck-fuck-fuck-fuck! I scratched green ribbons of innocent bark, twisting a broken branch on a wounded tendon, tearing and cursing, sinking my teeth into the budding stem, hammering with all my force until the young tree shook and bent, leant and with a slow rending crack snapped off just above the ground. In a boiling ecstasy I pinned it down, threshing and thrusting till the final sweet torture tore my secret essence from my scrotum and flooded the splintered passage. Even then I was unsatisfied, and getting up I began to break it to bits, snapping branches over my knee and spitting on them, throwing them as far as I could into the bushes. Then my mood shifted, and I took up a broken twig and gently smothered it with kisses. Later I carried it into a room full of undergraduates talking about God and threw it on the fire.

Enough! It is time to make my citadel.

LETTER FROM COUNCILLOR STRANGEWAYS TO THE CHIEF MEDICAL OFFICER OF HEALTH, MUNDHAM

Dear Dr Phillips,

I can only say that I am shocked and appalled by the imputations in your letter. As my good friend Mr Wilcox, our Sanitary Inspector, will have told you, Hooper Strangeways' record for cleanliness and hygiene is unsurpassed in the trade. We have, I would remind you, carried off the Gold Medallion at the Watford Exposition for four years running, and whilst my staff and I are only too anxious to co-operate with your department, I am afraid that it will not be possible, as you request, for analysts to inspect any part of the Plant. Many of the processes employed in the Treading Room and elsewhere are secret, and industrial espionage is becoming ever more common.

May I suggest, in all humility, that the reason the offensive substance mentioned in your letter was discovered in a bottle of Hooper Strangeways' Low-Calorie Burgundy was that the operative responsible for the analysis was negligent in the observance of fundamental personal hygiene precautions.

In answer to your queries about the other constituents used, couldn't we stop selling ourselves short for a change and give ourselves a bit of a pat on the back for one of the finest British products on the market? I myself have been drinking the stuff all my life and have never experienced any of the ill-effects you describe. In fact I have often blessed Hooper Strangeways Low-Calorie Burgundy as being responsible for my unvarying regularity, eight twenty-five and ten to six to be precise. If you have any further points to raise, please telephone me, but not at those times.

Yours sincerely,

A. Smith, for Councillor Strangeways.

EXCERPT FROM THE DIARY OF HUMPHREY MACKEVOY

Will they never leave me alone, even in prison? Normally life is very pleasant here. I get up at half-past seven, have breakfast in a corner of the canteen, and spend the morning cataloguing the library - an absurd task, but it takes my mind off other things - and Sellotaping torn pages. The Strangler rarely speaks, and then only to tell me pornographic anecdotes, and I have learned to smile in the right places without listening. After work I go for a walk. Someone has rescued Mummy's invalid chair, and now on

Sundays the men take turns at timing each other round the perimeter. I am officially allowed to go down to the village on Wednesday afternoons, but I have not done so. I am quite happy, though I find myself every day making a wider circle and treading a path nearer and nearer to the maples. I question, to amuse myself, if I were the kind of man who had sexual intercourse with trees, which one I would choose, and from which side. I always make the same choice. In the evenings I read in my room, usually the Bible. I cannot find my former way of life condemned even in the most stringent prohibitions of Leviticus. In short I am left to my own devices.

But this afternoon, after lunch, I was called to a room in the sick bay and asked to take my shoes, socks and uniform tunic off. I was then shown into another room with what looked like a very large old-fashioned sewing machine with a handle in one corner and a chair. Standing beside the machine was the lunatic Nipple in a white coat. I told him that I had no intention of being hypnotized again, as I was serving a sentence in which the punishment of psychiatry had not been prescribed by the Magistrate. Nipple went out of his way to be unctuous, and said that he wanted to offer me the chance of breaking the 'tree habit' as he called it. All he wanted me to do was to look at some pictures of trees and hold two pieces of wire connected to the machine. I am afraid that it must have been interest in what pictures he had to show me that made me stay, and I sat down in the chair in a resigned way and took the wires in my hands.

There was a music stand in front of the chair, and on it Nipple placed a picture of the Empire State Building, taken in the thirties with a caption underneath saying what it was. My heart sank, and I saw myself involved in some infantile party game which would lead inevitably to humiliation and wetting myself. I said I wanted to leave, but Nipple insisted that I should wait as there was something nice coming. The second picture showed a naked woman with her legs apart. I lost my temper and said I had had enough. I was just about to get up and go, when he hastily riffled through his pile of pictures and produced a heart-piercing Dürer engraving of a Linden tree, haunted by birds. Over the centuries I felt it needing me, turning its wanton flank for my eyes to caress. It was enough to make a man believe he had missed the Golden Age. Even the rough serge trousers I was wearing were poled up into a Bedouin tent as I allowed my eyes to follow Dürer's along the endlessly reflected patterns of the branches against the sky, the subtly-varied Ys that said You! You! You! While I was giving in to these temptations, I was vaguely aware of Nipple frenziedly turning the handle of his machine, and I felt a not unpleasant tingling sensation coming through the wires which he had asked me to hold. Suddenly, however, he gave a sharp cry and jumped back, shaking his hand.

I said the picture was very nice, and could I have it. He became abusive and started examining the machinery as though his life depended on it. When he had calmed down I asked him if he would show me another picture. Before doing so he went back to the machine, and turned the indicator of a large dial from 10 to 100. He then placed in front of me a colour photograph of the banyan tree, the ficus bene galensis. This is the Shiva of trees, with a thousand trunks, for the branches grow downwards and take root in the earth, making a private forest of themselves. I allowed my imagination to run lascivious riot: and whether it was from such long abstinence I do not know, but I felt myself jolted, convulsed with lewd excitement, my urethra a hot culvert of molten gold. In a way that I have never experienced before my hair stood on end, and such was the erotic violence of my phantom ejaculation that I felt myself lifted from the chair. It only lasted a moment but it was very beautiful.

Breathlessly I thanked Nipple, and felt grateful enough to ask him whether he had hurt himself. He said no, he had only given himself a mild electric shock. This prompted me to tell him about an accident at home, when one cold night, waking in the dark, Mummy had plugged her suspenders into the electric socket. At the word 'suspenders' Nipple inexplicably yelped, went rigid and leant against the wall holding his heart. I asked him what the matter was, and he begged me not to say 'that word'. I asked him which word, and he said 'suspenders'. The word was hardly out of his mouth when his face fixed in a rictous grin and he began to have convulsions, in the course of which he threw himself against the machine and apparently received another electric shock. My curiosity was aroused. ' Suspenders?' I asked. 'What's wrong with suspenders?' But by now he was threshing about on the floor like a landed fish, and I felt I should go and get help. An ambulance came for him an hour later.

I have finally brought myself to read the proofs of the Chaplain's book, *Jesus and the Red Planet*. It is, I am afraid, not to be his masterpiece. The story is seen through the eyes of Space Hostess Mary, who some years before had become pregnant after a mysterious encounter with a Being from outer space. Her child has now grown up, and is a pilot with Trans-Solar Spaceways. He proves himself from an early age to be a miraculous mechanic, mending computers with a touch of his hand, and lecturing tirelessly on the benefits of a new kind of rocket propellent of which tiny quantities are sufficient for intergalactic journeys. His experimental craft, 'New Covenant I', manned by a few loyal friends, is headed towards Mars when the perfidious navigator who is in the pay of the evil Rabbis, the strange inhabitants of the

Wandering Planet Zion, feeds false information into the computer. The spacecraft drifts while Jesus and his crew celebrate Moon Landing Day with their last vitamin pack. Shortly afterwards they fall into the gravitational pull of the Wandering Planet and are forced to land. They are taken prisoner by the Rabbis, armed with deadly Urims and Thummims, and are told that for aeons the Planet Zion has been the supplier of rocket propellent to the whole universe. Jesus's newfangled fuel has threatened their monopoly, and he must die.

They are taken with their craft in a Zionian articulated space transporter to a deserted corner of the universe, where Jesus is made to walk the plank. As he reaches the end the Zionian Rabbis cut his oxygen tube, and Jesus spirals silently away, arms outspread. The remaining disciples, minus Judas the Navigator who has exploded himself in a decompression chamber, are allowed to return to Earth. Entering the solar system, they are surprised by a knock on the window. Jesus comes in and shares their vitamin pills, and as they watch climbs out again through the hatch and zooms away in an unspecified direction. One day he may return and blow up the Planet Zion. In style the book leans heavily on the more lurid kinds of space comic, and most of the sayings of Jesus are reduced to monosyllabic expletives or long drawn-out cries, 'Vroom!' and 'Aaaaaaargh!' lingering longest in the memory.

I am just beginning a new exercise book, and looking back at entries a month ago I am shocked to see how quickly the pain of Labby's death is fading from that first obsessive grief. I am amazed at how soon my appetite for living has returned. Both my longing to be buried alive and my guilty sense of temptation have given way to an easier compromise. The question of my future after I leave here remains unresolved, but I am convinced that the only way I shall ever overcome my love for trees is by learning to love people more. I do not only mean in a sexual sense, though that must come first, but also in tolerance, and in a readiness to accommodate myself to society.*

LETTER FROM MISS ETHNE LONGRIDGE OM, DSO AND BAR TO INSPECTOR STONELEY

My dearest darling Fluff-Fluff,

Your Buzzie is giddy with happiness. I've completely got over the Ornithological Society disappointment, and Mrs Townsend can drink herself into the ground for all I care. Stage Four went without a hitch, didn't it. I can't tell you how frantic I was that everything should go well. I washed out both ears a dozen times, and all day today I wore my earmuffs in memory of your inquisitive little tongue. It didn't taste too waxy, did it? I should really have had them syringed. Stage Five is going to take a lot of thought, and perhaps a minor operation, but we'll jump that hurdle when we come to it.

Isn't it wonderful to feel well again, and, as you so sweetly said, much lighter. The plumbers' men were here again today at last and dug up the garden. I almost begged them to let me have your trousers, but they were in a sorry state I'm afraid. What a ghastly month we've all had with this tummy thing! Taking up sex so late in life it was agony not to be able to press ahead.

Ursie is still very groggy I'm sorry to say, but thank God for Florrie. Ever since she got back from seeing Humphrey she's been a tower of strength. Her theory is that Smart is poisoning us all slowly in revenge for being squashed by the

* This resolve reflects itself in the entries for this period which I have not included here. There is much discussion of the weather with other prisoners and information about football matches.

Council over the spraying. Personally I agree with you that it must have been something in the wine. After all it's only the sort of people who drink wine who have become so ill. Did you hear that Bee Gross had died? I'm so glad about the raid on Strangeways'. When is it to happen? And do, my dearest darling, be careful, I so abhor the thought of your being hurt.

Which leads me to the next thing. When I think of your poor bottom criss-crossed with welts I'm tortured with guilt. Is it really necessary, Reggie? You're not a delinquent at all, and never have been, even without regular spankings: you're a good, kind, conscientious, hard-working police inspector. I've been looking at those new canes you bought, Reggie. They're sharp. One's even got little tintacks stuck in it. Surely that can't be good for you! We must have a chat about this. Meanwhile I'm doing the exercises you suggested for my forehand, and I've even borrowed Florrie's dumb-bells.

Golly, what a strong woman she is! At the moment she's practising lifting weights under water in the bath with some sort of breathing apparatus, and doing bird whistles for a mysterious pet she's got in a basket in the garden. She says could you be an angel and bring her some gelignite next time you come round? Yesterday she proved a tremendous boon in helping me electrify the hems of my underwear. You can't see the little wires, they're hidden in the lace. And the batteries are in a place where you can't get at them, you naughty man! I think this should ensure the success of Stages Five and Six, however impulsive you are, mad Fluff-Fluff.

Little kisses,

Buzzie.

EXCERPT FROM THE DIARY OF HUMPHREY MACKEVOY

I have made friends with another prisoner, a Mr Spence, an ex-bank-manager whose table I sat at for breakfast. He has only one topic of conversation, which is how many times he has managed to masturbate the night before. He then describes in great detail the fantasties which accompany what he calls 'pulling his pud', and expects me, I think, to do the same.

He begins every night by imagining that he has just arrived in his office, whereupon every member of his staff, male and female, young and old, are required to perform disgusting duties on him in order of seniority. He then goes through the day having similar experiences with each of his customers under threat of refusing them an overdraft. One figure that crops up again and again is a Japanese heavyweight wrestler, on tour in this country and temporarily out of funds.

This morning, while in the middle of one of these descriptions, he became so agitated that he had to go away to the lavatory. His skin is a shocking colour, and he has purple-black rings under his eyes. His hands shake, and I cannot believe it is good for his health.*

LETTER FROM MRS CHAS SMART TO DR ROBERTS

Egregious Doctor.

I write to you about my husband. He is gone mad. He is refused to take the Pills you have give him and sit all day

---

* This extract is representative of twenty others in which I wrote down the fruits of my overtures to other prisoners. Seen in the mass they convince me that it was my repugnance both at the form and content of their solitary sexual indulgence that made me feel less guilty about my own fantasies, increasingly numerous now, about trees real and imaginary.

eating the figs and drinking olive oil. Early in the morning he go out and come back very disgusting. I an beg you please, Doctor, come to us again. What he do last time he do not mean. Everyday I see my husband become thin like a man who has been dead. His hair fall out, he is white as the cheese and he no say nothing to me. What have we done that God send us this?

I beg you to have pity.

Your servant,

Pia Smart.

EXCERPT FROM THE DIARY OF HUMPHREY MACKEVOY

Christmas Day. The happiest Christmas for years, even if it is the first without Labby. I attended Matins in the canteen. Some of the girls in the kitchen were drunk, and pushed balloons up their skirts to suggest they were pregnant. At a pre-arranged signal during a pause in the sermon one of the older women asked them in a loud voice who the father was, and they pointed at Mr Luff. The sermon, which took the form of a tactical retreat from the Virgin Birth, ended in a rout, drowned by their shouts of raucous laughter. For my fellow-prisoners the day has obviously been a sad one. In keeping with my resolution to be more sociable I have tried to be cheery, but I was met with blank self-pity.

For my part I think I shall try and be in prison every Christmas. The memory of Christmases with Mummy suffocates me. I am sure it was her sincere wish to give me 'a real Christmas', but since Daddy disappeared it has obviously been a lugubrious undertaking for her. She would begin at breakfast by wondering with a sigh how we should spend the day, in a tone that implied that the hours to come were some un-negotiable foreign currency. The turkey was always twice the capacity of the oven and devilled legs were often eaten as late as Shrove Tuesday. Hidden from each other by the carcase in the middle of the table we would sit in thoughtful silence. I used to wonder on what safari it had been captured: where she got them I do not know, but they tasted like elephant flesh. She would sit weeping behind the turkey, complaining that there was still the Christmas pudding and the mince pies to eat, and that she didn't know how we should get through it all. In the afternoon we would play Murder, and after tea we would settle down to an evening of lachrymose indigestion.

It will be different this year. Now that she has tapped new sources of vitality I imagine she is out after Smart, prowling the streets and waiting her opportunity to strike. There are times when I am sorry for him.

EXCERPT FROM THE INTIMATE JOURNAL OF ROSE HOPKINS

Barry had an accident this afternoon and it was touch and go. One thing that has gone is part of his thing. He was playing 'Chicken' with some other boys at school with the paper guillotine in the Dark Room when it happened. Michael Bachelor who was working the handle said he just didn't jump back quick enough. I am so lucky. The doctor told Michael that it was not as serious as they thought at first and it only nicked his foreskin. Michael Bachelor has been expelled and the Dark Room is out of bounds. Dad is very pleased, and bought me four bags of crisps. But it is cruel that this should happen before Barry did it properly. He nearly did it in the Regal last Saturday morning during *The Bells of St Mary's*, but he got nervy because of the lady in the row behind who was telling me to stop it, and then he got his cramps again. Those damn cramps! I put an ice-cream down his trousers and he felt much better. But from now on I am going to nurse him and love him for himself.

147

We will be married and spend all day with no clothes on and do it all the time. Sometimes he looks just like Kenneth More.

EXCERPT FROM THE DIARY OF HUMPHREY MACKEVOY

I tried to talk to Mr Voyce again this morning. We, or rather he, had a long conversation about his wife's budgerigar which apparently has some kind of liver trouble and has gone deaf. But all the time he was talking I found myself staring past his steaming mouth at the maple. I was happy in the knowledge that I could do without it. It taunted me, but I had systematically, over a single year, by dint of much travelling to aboretums and botanical gardens, enjoyed the whole family of maples, the *Aceraceae*: the *acer macrophyllum* the big-leafed maple, a round-headed tree that can grow up to a hundred feet in height, with fragrant yellow flowers and leaves a foot across; the *acer palmatum* the Japanese maple - the one I fucked was barely a shrub - its leaves scarlet that autumn, in shape like those of a rococo sycamore; the *acer spicatum*, the mountain maple, its flowers greenish-yellow, the colour of absinth and forgetfulness; the *acer saccharinum*, the silver maple that I damaged in the Arboretum at Nottingham, with finer, softer wood than the rest of its family, its long-stalked, deeply-lobed, coarsely-toothed leaves green above and greyish white beneath; the acer cappadocicum, the coliseum maple, whose young branches are a lustrous green: the red red sugar maple, acer saccharum, and the remarkable acer griseum, the paper-bark maple from Western China, then snug in the Gardens at Kew, with its beautiful rich cinnamon-brown bark exposing the wood beneath in curling torn strips of tactile delights.

The one I was staring at was the common Norwegian maple, *acer platanoides*. I had had hundreds of them.

Mr Voyce was saying that the budgerigar's real trouble lay in its knees, and that it had taken for several months to lying on its back with its feet in the air and refusing food. Again I found myself thinking what strange partners I have had in the heaving darkness, strangest of all perhaps the sausage tree, *kigelia pinnata*, a native of Africa, with its foul-scented flowers that open at night and those strange sausage-shaped fruit that defy the strongest teeth; the devil tree, *alstonia scholaris*, the wood of whose dropsical trunk was once used for writing-tablets in Asia, but on which I wrote another message: the traveller's tree, *revenala madagascariensis*, a peacock's tail of palms that swayed like a giant punkalla under my urgent heavings; *brachychiton rupestsris* the barrel tree, my honey pot, with cooling water stored beneath the bark, and a sweet edible jelly that I sucked from the wound during our monstrous foreplay; the cannon ball tree, *couroupita guianensis*, that I shagged in the Botanical Gardens in Oxford, matching my testicles to its globular woody fruit, each one eight inches across, and trampling the rank-smelling fallen gourds beneath my feet.

Far away Mr Voyce remarked how odd it was that his wife should be suffering from the same symptoms as her budgerigar. In my mind the vast army of my conquests marched towards and through me, headed by the Praetorian Guard of the Gymnosperms, evergreens and conifers. Their very name, scrotal and gymnastic at once, caressed my genitals. These red-wooded giants, skirted with layered green needles, heavy with phallic cones, scented with resin, heroes of the Mesozoic Age, and the *ginkgo biloba*, whose leaves are likened by the English to maidenhair, by the Germans to the symbol of sexual union, and by the Chinese to a duck's foot. And the suburban chilean pine, *araucaria araucana*, whose pinate bifurcations are rumoured to puzzle the monkey: but not me!

Then the Angiosperms – again the mysterious eroticism of their name touched my sensitive sac – the whole company of trees, first among them the *monocotyledons*, whose flowers part in threes or multiples of three; *pandanus*, the screw-pine, deliciously named and sweetly scented, so often inaccessible by reason of the stilt-roots against the trunk; the exotic fronded palms, the *principes*, with their rutted, hairy trunks fecund with sago and oil: among them the raffia palm, *raphia ruffia*, whose flowers emerge from among the leaves and branch into enormous centipedes with their seedpods set regularly in two rows, like trousers to the centipedes' legs, twelve feet long and hanging menacingly over the head of the lover.

Then among the angiosperms, the dicotyledons, whose flowers part in fours and fives: the fluffy, teasing cottonwood, *populus deltoides*, the aspen, the weeping willow, *salix babylonica*, and its sister *salix matsudana tortuosa*, the permanent wave tree, like a tree seen through a haze of heat: the shagbark hickory, *carya nata*, to me the dearest and the most exciting of the *juglandales* (from *jovis glans*, Jove's acorn) of the family of the walnut and the pecan. The *betulaceae*, the erotic plenty of the world, alders and silver birches, tasselled with polleny catkins, hornbeams and hazels. The beeches, *fagaceae*, attractive at all seasons of the year with an unyielding hard-edged wood that bites at the pelvis. The oaks, the ancient English oak, *quercus robur*, my first taste of Nature's bounty, the evergreen oak, *quercus virginiana*, with a branch spread of as much as one hundred and fifty feet, and the great meadow-caressing *quercus ilex*, the holm oak, and not to be forgotten, the shy *quercus pubescens*, the pubescent oak, whose bitter-tasting leaves are hairy on the undersides.

The elms next, *urticales*, the most highly developed in the evolutionary line, with tiny sophisticated leaves that mock the antediluvian primitives of frond and needle; the mulberries, and the deadly upas tree, *antiaris toxicaria*, about which such extravagant and malicious tales have been told; the breadfruit, *artocarpus communis*, the Grail of Captain Bligh, and the fig, whose leaves have made for me erotic accessories to many a tedious marble.

Angiosperms too. The sandalwood, *santalum album*, a fragrant dream of India, shafted by moonlight in the Botanical Garden at Inverewe, in windy Sutherland; the pokeweed, *phytolacca dioca*, hollow but clean of insects the tulip tree, *liriodendron tulipilera*, I had the luck to have in fragrant flower in the West of Ireland; and the primitive magnolia of full-blown waxy blooms. The exotic Malay ylang-ylang, *cananga odoratum*, whose blossoms were crushed to make Macassar Oil in Victoria's England; the nutmeg, *myristica fragrans*, for the sake of which the King of Spain's daughter came to visit the writer of that Tudor nursery rhyme, and the laurel that the ancients believed imparted poetic inspiration and the gift of prophecy: I am never more inventive than with one of their species; the cloud canyons of perfumed angels' wings I have dreamed of in the lubricated cleft of its sister, *cinnamonum camphora*, the camphor tree, prove the substance of that antique myth. And the cinnamon itself is spiced beyond description.

The hazel, the plane tree and the toothsome gums, I have enjoyed them all. The hawthorn and the Persian quince, cydonia, the Romans' tree of happiness. The loquat, the guara, the plum, and the harlot finery of the flowering cherry, *prunus serrulata*; the thorny acacia, dangerous to love, but graceful and burdened with blossoms; the *acacia acuminata* with its freshly-bored wood smelling of raspberry jam; the spikey honey-locust, *gleditsia triacanthos*, with flowering cruel thorns, and the same genus is graced by the laburnum, *laburnum anagyroides*, my Labby, distinguished by its fatal fruit. Sweet poison of which I drank and drank! Oh those silky, pubescent leaves, the golden chains in which I glory even now. The rain tree, *samanea saman*, poised in the earth with sinuous heavy boughs, the rose-red budded tamarind, the lemon, the lime, the sour orange, and the cork tree, *phellodendron*, that I went to Spain to visit, next to the incredible balsa, *ochroma pyramidale*, the most fragile fuck of them all, and the hop, *ptelia trifoliata*, on which I was so nearly caught.

Ailanthus then, my Tree of Heaven, and *swietenia*, the dark mahogany with its greenish yellow flowers, the evergreen boxwood, pink-leaved mago and the holly that punctures the bare buttocks; the horse-chestnut, *aesculus hippocastanum* mistakenly named by Matthioli, doctor to Maximilian II, in 1565 when he was told that the Turks fed their horses on conkers, and taken into the Greek by Linnaeus himself, my mentor and Michelin.

The Chinese jujube, *zizyphus jujuba*, growing its thorns in pairs, one curved and one straight: the sea hibiscus with brilliant yellow flowers, maroon-centred, that live only for a day; the giant baobab, whose grotesque beauty I can only face in certain moods; the mighty bombax, *bombax nialabaricum*, the red silk cotton tree, and *theobroma cacao*, the chocolate tree, known to the Incas and mother of Mars Bars and Cadbury's Flake; the tamarisk and Governor's plum from Madagascar and the myrtle, whose leaves were pierced by Phaedra waiting for Hippolytus and which is itself Myrrha, mother of Adonis, changed into a tree for her unnatural love for her father.

Shall I describe the bottle-brush and the koala-bear-haunted eucalyptus, the sticky and wooly-butt, *eucalyptus iongifolia*, the clown-white ghost gum, and the shady coolabah tree beneath which I did more than boil my billy? The flowering dogwood, *cornus florida*? The milky mimusops, the ebony, *diospyros ebenum*, against whose rock-hard heartwood I have stubbed myself and cried out in sleeping Kew? The fringe tree, the epaulette tree, the ash and the olive, *olea euro paea*, the teak and the strychnine, *strychnus nuxvomica*? The yellow oleander and the doghane, the figwort and verbena, catulpa and jacaranda? No, I will not. Custom cannot stale their infinite variety. I will name only a tree that I have it not in my heart to love. The rubber tree, *hevea brasiliensis*, whose tiny blossoms are admittedly seductive. But I have approached it twice, and each time only escaped after an immense effort from the gluey latex.

As I thought of the rubber tree I became aware that Mr Voyce had gone, and that I was still staring at the maple, *acer platanoides*, standing with its companions against the barbed wire.

CUTTING FROM THE *Mundham Advertiser*

> HOPKINS-SAVAGE: Mr and Mrs Arthur Hopkins, of 34 Brickwood Lane, Mundham, announce the engagement of their daughter, Rose, to Barry, only son of Captain and Mrs E. M. Savage of the Salvation Army Citadel, Mundham. The wedding will take place quietly on Tuesday next at the Mundham Registrar's Office.

> *Deaths*

> BROWNLOW. Suddenly at her home on Monday, Bridget Martha ('Midge') dearly beloved daughter of Mrs Redcliffe Brownlow of the Dyke, Sappho Close, Guildford.

TELEGRAM TO MR CHARLES SMART, ANONYMOUS

CONGRATULATIONS ON SUCCEEDING WITH ARSON WANTON
DESTRUCTION TREE MURDER AND BAREFACED
EMBEZZLEMENT STOP ENJOY IT WHILE YOU CAN STOP THE
MASKED WOMAN

EXCERPT FROM THE MUNDHAM POLICE STATION BEAT
INFORMATION BOOK

Operation Pluto

Pursuant on allegations made by the Chief Medical Officer
of Health for Mundham, Dr E. Phillips, in connection with
the recent gastritis epidemic and the continuing non-
cooperation of Councillor Strangeways in the matter of
permitting any inspection of his factory at Hooper
Strangeways Ltd it was decided with the approval of CID
Reading to mount a police raid on the above premises to be
known under the code name Operation Pluto.

Keys to the premises were obtained by Mr Charles
Smart who has a nodding acquaintance with Mrs F. C.
Pollock, an operative in the Hooper Strangeways' Bottling
Plant, and a detachment under the command of Inspector
Stoneley, accompanied by Mr Smart and Dr E. Phillips left
the Police Station at 21.00 hrs on the night of February 2nd.

Any subsequent official enquiry into the circumstances
of this tragic night should bear in mind the still unexplained
phenomena which began to crop up at an early stage. A mile
or so down the Reading Road, Mr Smart, who was sitting in
the front of the Police Wolseley 9090, began to throw
himself about in his seat. The car was brought to a stop, and
as the nearside door was opened a large hooded snake was

seen to slip away into the undergrowth. Pursuit was made, but no trace of the reptile could be found. Constable Mohammed reported hearing a series of low whistles, but nothing was found. How the snake got into the car remains a mystery.

Mr Smart, though unhurt, was understandably alarmed, and spoke several times – and this may have a bearing on subsequent events – of a 'terrible woman'. Owing to Mr Smart's state of fear, it was necessary to stop on four further occasions before reaching the factory.

On arrival it was discovered that Sgt Makins and Constable Pearmain had already arrived and had established radio contact with Headquarters in Reading. Makins, who had refrained from forcing an entry pending the arrival of the main force, reported seeing Councillor Strangeways' face at a window some minutes before, clearly distressed.

An entry was effected, and the party, led by Inspector Stoneley, crossed the dispatch shed towards the Managing Director's Office. At this moment a barrel became dislodged from an overhead rack and burst on the floor, narrowly missing Mr Smart. Foul play was at first suspected, but on inspection the loft was revealed to have been empty.

On reaching the Managing Director's Office, it was found that the door was locked from the inside. Hearing no reply to a challenge, Constable Mohammed then forced the door. Councillor Strangeways was found lying on the floor, still holding in his hand an open tin of Hooper's 'Rat Doom'. Dr Phillips examined the body and determined that death had occurred within the last ten minutes. A sealed note addressed 'To whom it may concern' was found near the body, and on being opened discovered to contain the words 'It is just one damn thing after another.'

On the finding of the body, Mr Smart became excitable, dancing about the room clapping his hands and laughing, and had to be restrained from kicking the corpse. On proceeding to the Vat Room, leaving Sgt Makins to guard the Managing Director's Office, Mr Smart, though in a very sickly condition, ran in front. By the time police reached the room he was already dragging himself up the ladder to the main vat, where despite police orders to come down, he began to deliver a speech blackening the character of the deceased and claiming that Mundham had been cleansed of evil. Mr Smart then turned towards the vat, shouted the words 'Oh! No! The Mask!' and fell in.

Constable Pearmain immediately climbed the ladder and succeeded in pulling Mr Smart out. Dr Phillips gave first aid, but was of the opinion that due to Mr Smart's weakened condition there was little hope for his life. An ambulance was called but Mr Smart expired some minutes before it arrived. Both bodies were taken to the Police Mortuary pending an Inquest. It was my own opinion that the drowned man's behaviour was brought about by delusions arising from chronic gastritis, and Dr Phillips will attest in the same vein. Sample bottles of the Hooper Strangeways product were also taken for analysis, and Sgt Makins was left on duty in the premises. It is my duty to record that during the night Sgt (now Constable) Makins became inebriated as a result of drinking the Managing Director's Port and returned to the Station without waiting to be relieved, with confused reports of having heard a mysterious slapping sound and having found the wet tracks of a very large duck leading from the main vat to the door of the dispatch shed. A search was made and no trace of any such trail was to be discovered.*

* The newspaper report of these events presented the story in a rather different light, Strangeways allegedly having committed

LETTER FROM MISS KOCH TO HUMPHREY MACKEVOY

Dear Humphrey!

You know that I have never made demands on you, but why, please Humphrey, have you not written? What have I done that you do not write to me?

For two months I have been so ill, Humphrey, and every day I have written to you.‡ Finally I have got an old German remedy from a bottle of Piesporter Auslese, and since then all is well. But I am holding my thumbs.

Oh Humphrey, why do you do these things to me? When you see Albuhera Walk you will be surprised! Your room I have made all new, very modern, with our big bed. I have knitted a coverlet and hot water bottle bags, and I keep all my make-up and undergarments in your bathroom. It is so cosy, Humphrey.

I have placed next to our bed the creche of our baby, so that we may lie in bed and imagine him there, crying perhaps or needing to be changed. I know you will do it with love, Humphrey. How I imagine things! I think we shall call him Klaus. I have written to my parents in Schweinfurt, and do you know, they want to come and live with us! My father plays the accordion and has a collection of more than four hundred pipes. You will love him,

suicide due to overwork, and Smart having died at his home of pneumonia. The obituaries filled an entire page of the Advertiser and described them as turbulent twins, vying with one another in their service to the community. The findings of the Public Analyst were suppressed and the victims, with the exception of Mrs Gross, gradually recovered. The firm of Hooper Strangeways was apparently on the edge of bankruptcy, and the factory now makes an equally poisonous children's sugar drink under a new management. H.M.

‡ This is true. H.M.

Humphrey, I know it. And my mother is such a jolly, big woman, with a most powerful voice. Just think, Humphrey! With my father playing the accordion we can sing together in the evenings. And your dear Mama can sing with us.

She is very merry today, and splashing in the bath with her frog costume and oxygen gas tank. How she makes us laugh!

Guess what! Miss Longridge is to be married like us, but it is a secret.

Your own,

Ursula.

EXCERPT FROM THE DIARY OF HUMPHREY MACKEVOY

The line between fantasy and reality, like the frontier of a beleaguered state, is tortuous and deeply indented: the land on either side of where one stands may be foreign, yet the salient of one's own aggression remains illogically safe. It is also sown with mines and watched over by machine-gun towers. Tonight I crossed that line, and at what expense!

I have often mused on the maple trees by the barbed wire, and tonight I allowed myself a mental stroll towards them. So accurate has been my imagination in the past, so precise the sensation of crushing the grass under my feet, of hearing the early hooting of an owl, the distant clatter of a train in the gathering darkness, that when, moments later, I found myself actually on that walk, the transition was uncanny. I was stepping it out confidently, as though I had nowhere in particular in the world to go: Only my hand in my pocket, filled now and restraining, told me of my unacknowledged purposes.

The compound was deserted. A showing of *The Conquest of Everest* in the canteen had drawn my fellow-prisoners from their onanistic exercises, and sliding coloured shadows flickered at the windows of the building. I tried to imagine that I was dreaming, handing off the moral responsibility and knowing that even if the dream ended in shame I could forgive myself and turn to the wall with a sense of uncomplicated relief. Holding myself like a sleep-walker and closing my eyes, I almost fell into the foundations of the church. I stopped. This was no justified fantasy, but an unjustifiable flirtation with moral danger. I walked on.

I touched the first maple and the old electricity sent my meters mad. I withdrew my hand. Breathing deeply to still the pounding of my heart, I gazed at the sky and heard a roar of laughter from the canteen. My hand stole back. After a second's mossy exploration I sniffed at my finger-tips, and was thrilled to find that lack of practice had not dulled the sharpness of my perception. I could still distinguish beneath the musk the light sappy growth smell, and my nostrils for a moment became boudoirs of moss-lined, leaf-carpeted treehollow.

Panting now, I transferred my fingers to my mouth, and sucked greedily at the faint smear. In a cold instant I was revulsed. It was as if the Laburnum had whispered my name. In a frenzy of remorse I smashed my hand against the bole of the maple, and went on banging it until it was numb. The fragile bones cracked against one another and the pain was so great that I tucked it wincing under my armpit. To my horror my other hand, possessed, it seemed, of its own desires, began its spidery insinuations. I was powerless to stop it, as the stronger of my two hands was now out of action. Or so I allowed myself to believe.

Quick as a squirrel it scampered up the trunk, a glissando through scales of pleasure that filled my whole body with music, brushing feathery trills from the satin smooth bark, scattering brisk arpeggios of dirty mindedness. My brain told me this was only the overture, and against my will my clumsy right hand leapt to begin the first act: the first unbuttoning. It took time. Time enough, I admit, to reconsider, to draw back, to do up my trousers and go back to the hut. But my injured hand was no match for the bounding jab of my heavyweight member. Bole, trunk, branches, twigs, twigs, branches, trunk, bole! My hands flew down again and gripped, forcing my member flat against the trunk, so that I could feel each rut and contusion along its length. I bit, licked, kissed and floated into a calm bay of liquid languor.

A cough behind my back shrivelled me. It was the nightmare of Paradise Woods all over again. I made a maladroit pretence of signalling a completed evacuation of the bladder by shaking my member vigorously and stowing it in my trousers. I turned round. The Chaplain was kneeling on the grass a few feet away, his fingers interlaced, his head bent in prayer. It is rare to experience shame in a prison: the fear of social opprobrium has been removed. I in my turn cleared my throat. He looked up, smiling, and congratulated me fervently. 'Hello,' he said, 'I've been praying for you. No one can stop birds perching on their head, but we can stop them nesting there.'

I was not prepared to follow him into the labyrinth of theological imagery, and I began to trudge back to the hut, utterly drained of any emotion. The Chaplain loped at my heels like a big dog, occasionally slapping me on the back, and doing his best to cheer me up by suggesting that I had won a great victory. What persuaded me to go back to his room with him for a cup of cocoa I shall never know. On the way there I allowed him to conduct me through the imaginary West Door of his church. We then picked our way through the litter-strewn foundations to the unbroken earth where, he assured me, the high altar would one day stand. He suggested that the next time I felt tempted by desire I should divert my excitement into a worthier channel, by turning out with pick and spade to dig among the earthworks.

His room was hot and stuffy. On the bed was an awl and some strips of leather; he appeared to have been making a gunbelt and holsters. Round the walls were the sort of crude paintings one might find in an infants' school, on curling yellow paper attached with Sellotape, showing scenes from the life of Jesus by a prisoner whose imagination had been kindled by the Chaplain's Wild West analogies. While the milk was heating on a gas-ring he compared me to St Anthony, and then to an international footballer who had resisted the temptation to kick the goalkeeper and would be rewarded by a clear shot at goal some minutes later that would bring the terraces to their feet in acclamation.

As we drank our cocoa he continued in similar vein, saying that this was a celebration, and repeating the words 'Hooray for you! Yes, yes!' as he fumbled about the room looking for some biscuits. Those he found were chocolate-covered and had been in the tin a very long time. He told me that I was not alone in being tempted. He himself frequently felt the desire to go to Hollywood, ring up Rita Hayworth, and give her 'a good do' behind the studios.

I became paralysed with despair: the thought that in a few days I should be free terrified me. I was neither grateful nor resentful to the Chaplain for having prevented me from giving way to temptation: the ache of unfulfilled desire and the pain of guilt were indistinguishable. I stared at a misshapen, discarded holster lying under the bed and thought, while the Chaplain's bright exhortations flew past overhead in formation, that once I was free it would always be one or the other: somewhere a tree would be left alone or left ravaged. It would be withered frustration or grief, with no Chaplain to intervene and impose a specious armistice.

Through this despair I heard the Chaplain asking me what it was about trees that made me want to 'do' them. There was then silence. No one had ever asked me this, and I was first too shocked to speak. He was quick to reassure me, and said that he hadn't meant to ask what it was about trees that made me want to 'do' them, but why I did it. However determined I was not to answer I found the second silence invincible. I finally said very quietly that I made love to trees because I was what I was: but I would never do it again.

The Chaplain beamed his pleasure at my renunciation, and said that he was sure I had put my trees behind me, but the next time I found myself as dangerously close to 'cracking' as I had been earlier in the evening I should remember that God looked kindly on the masturbator. What was needed was a safety-valve. He went to a cupboard and brought out a twisted mass of metal with a black handle protruding from it. This, he said, had once been a pressure cooker which had blown up in his sister's flat, all because its safety-valve had become clogged with a piece of cabbage. This could happen to a man too, he said. He forced me to take it and examine it, and told me that he had often produced it with great success during his sermons.

He asked me if I ever imagined myself 'doing' a tree. I nodded, and confessed that there was scarcely a tree that I could not immediately picture in my mind in that context. He was delighted. Fantasies, he explained, were close relatives of art. He cited Shakespeare, Galsworthy and Somerset Maugham, picturing them lying in bed at night and weaving imaginary adventures round the names of Portia, Irene, and Miss Sadie Thompson. There was nothing to be ashamed of, because no harm could be done to anyone, least of all to oneself, if reasonable care was taken.

Self-abuse was a misnomer. It was rather self-use. He tentatively asked whether I knew the technique involved, and offered to lend me a pamphlet published by the Anglo–Catholic Truth Society entitled *Masturbation: a handbook*.

I was very embarrassed by the topic he was discussing, and more so by the foetid blush that had spread over the Chaplain's neck and face as he strained to talk to me man to man. I promised to read the pamphlet, and clumsily got up to go. I had reached the front door before I realized that there was something else he wanted to talk about. He said that he had begun a new book portraying Jesus as a lumberjack. I had the impression that he had invented the analogy for my benefit. He outlined the plot of this extravagant excursion, explaining that Jesus as an old man emigrates to Canada where in the thick forests of the Rocky Mountains he comes upon the Pharisee Brothers, a band of lazy lumberjacks lounging about their sordid encampment licking maple syrup and dandling on their knees female refugees from the brothels of the Yukon Gold Rush.

Their sloth has allowed the forest to reoccupy the clearings and the fields painfully carved out by the settlers, and the giant trees had grown together at their tops, blotting out the light. Jesus sets about the trees with his favourite axe, called Love, and by his example encourages the settlers to restore order and fruitfulness to their land. After an epic log-rolling contest with the elder of the Pharisee Brothers, Jesus falls victim to a piece of sleight of foot and is lost to sight in the boiling white water among the black baulks of timber. The Chaplain asked me if I would be willing to help him with the descriptive passages. I was left with the impression that he sees it as a therapeutic exercise, and hopes that by encouraging me to collaborate in a book hostile to trees he will influence me against them.

I almost wish he stood a chance of success. Sitting here

in my cell with the pamphlet open in front of me at an illustration of Mendelssohn being introduced to Queen Victoria, I know my case is hopeless. I shall never lose my love for the smell of trees in the summer, or the desire to touch them, caress them, possess them. In my waking dreams I shall return to them again and again, revisiting all my former conquests in turn, and planning spectral variations of seduction and rape, hazy juxtapositions that I float through in sleepy surges of desire. These are my fantasies.

But the reality will be different. Catching sight of myself in a mirror, the veins standing out on my forehead, I shall see the difference: between the sexual hero of my many-coloured dreams, triumphant in solitude, and the lonely man on the lavatory seat, crouched over a piston fist. Nor is it any comfort, as the handbook suggests, to imagine myself as a member of the great global brotherhood – and, I was surprised to learn, sisterhood – of masturbators. From the igloos of the icecap where the Eskimo, dumpy in his furs, sits straining by the blubber lamp, down through the tundra, where by his grazing horse the Cossack, huddled behind a windbreak, struggles to hold the image of his gypsy love against the howling gale, to the Congo where a plump Chieftain turns his sad eyes to the straw roof in the cicada-riven dusk, and the banks of the Ganges where the turbaned Swami of the prominent rib-cage balances on his head, dreaming of the hundred-breasted Goddess and falls over with an exhausted sigh. To say nothing of the millions in silent tenements in the concrete cities of the world: the galley-slaves of habit, beating a sad insistent rhythm, rowing the night towards dawn.

And yet. The other reality is unbearable. To become attached to another tree as I became attached to the Laburnum would be not only a betrayal, it would damage the tree and myself. I learned tonight how easy it is to cross the line: how monstrous a fantasy can become if it is realized. I vowed when Labby was felled that I would not touch another tree for the rest of my life: I renew that vow every night as I fall asleep.

I will never fuck a tree again.

LETTER FROM MISS KOCH TO HUMPHREY MACKEVOY

My dearest Humphrey!

In one week you will be with me! In forty weeks perhaps our little Klaus, our small manchild, will be opening his blue eyes to the daylight. What a birthday that will be!

Oh, Humphrey, why have you not written to me? Each morning I go on foot to meet the Post Man. He is very friendly, but never, Humphrey, never has he had a letter for me. He has a big moustache and such a wicked smile.

Imagine! My father has given up his position with the Railway, and our mother has sold the little house in Schweinfurt! Soon, I think, we shall all be together!

Come quickly, Humphrey! In the streets the people are so happy now that Mr Smart and Mr Strangeways are under the ground! People speak of you too, Humphrey, and they believe that you were a good man, as do I.

I love you so much. On Monday morning I shall stand for hours in the garden with arms outstretched waiting until you come round the corner and embrace me. Till then, my dearest, store your passion for me carefully!

Your own,

Ursie.

EXCERPT FROM THE DIARY OF HUMPHREY MACKEVOY

I have spent my last day in prison putting things straight in the library. No doubt in a week or two most of my work will have been undone and it will be in the same shocking mess that it was in when I found it. But this evening at least everything was perfectly spick and span. I have introduced pink cards for Westerns, white for Pornography, and blue for Theology, and also completed a cross-index of titles and authors' names. At my suggestion the Strangler has sponged and Sellotaped all the damaged pages, and made brown paper jackets for those in particularly bad condition. It is nothing like the Shop, but it is unrecognizably better than it was when I came here. I have even succeeded in having the offensive female nude calendar removed and a coloured reproduction of 'Autumn in the Forest' by Edgar Smyth put up in its place. The Chaplain was good enough to say that I had found the library all brick and had left it all marble.

I was very touched when the Strangler came over at closing time with a paperweight in the form of a glass globe mounted on a black plastic base and containing a snow-storm round a lighthouse at sea. He said that he had enjoyed our conversations and was sorry to see me go. It was the same in the canteen this evening. As is the custom, everyone gave up their pudding for me, with the result that I had to eat twentythree bowls of suet pudding and custard under the benevolent gaze of my fellow-prisoners and am now paying the penalty for it. I was also able to thank the canteen ladies, one of whom tried to kiss me. The bank manager stepped up to me on the way to my hut - he has stopped coming to supper in the canteen - gave me a limp hand and begged me to send him certain magazines.

After lunch I had my final interview with the Governor. He has made very little impression on me while I have been here. He has very little to do with the men, and is obsessed with trying to breed a tortoiseshell budgerigar. I found him cleaning out their cage with a toothbrush, and their soft cheeping and the presence of one of them - a turquoise blue - sitting on his head distracted me throughout our brief interview. He told me he was sure that I would be coming back to see them, and asked me to remember that as I went out into the world people would be watching me. I was to think of myself as an ambassador for Droxford. He begged me not to let the prison down. After a few moments the Governor's wife, who had been searching for an escaped budgerigar up the chimney, emerged with a handful of sooty feathers clenched in her fist. She favoured me with a flashing smile and went next door for a shower.

The Governor said that a lot of people used Droxford as a place to escape to out of the terrifying hurly-burly of life, but they couldn't stay here for ever. He wished they could, but sooner or later everybody had to learn to stand on their own feet. At this point the budgerigar's tail lifted, and a black and white viscous lump of droppings detached itself and began to slide like a glacier down the Brylcreemed slopes of his head. Lightened, the bird flew off and perched on a huge wall-chart, seeming to mock its diagrammatic progression of colour blocks from white to tortoiseshell.

At the end of our interview the Governor picked up the telephone and asked for my clothes to be brought in, and a moment later his wife returned in her dressing-gown, carrying my tweed suit and my Veldschoen tucked under her arm. Then she erected an ironing board, spat on the iron, and began to iron my shirt, underpants and tie as if she harboured a grudge against them.

Tomorrow morning I shall put that suit on for the first time after so many months of blue dungarees. I have no clear idea where I shall be going. The Governor suggested

New Zealand. The prospect of walking again in the streets of Mundham, of being looked at and whispered about, of being the centre of a scandal, even the instigator of a chain of events which ended in more than one death, is unbearable: to go home at night through that garden, and to have to pass the shattered stump…To say nothing of Miss Koch, poor girl. I have written to Mummy to try and explain.

For once I feel no sexual desire at all.

LETTER FROM MISS KOCH TO HUMPHREY MACKEVOY

Oh Humphrey!

You do not love me! Often I have suspected it but now I know it! That you have not written to me but to your Mother I understand, but what a letter! How can you suggest to your dear Mama that you cannot come home because I will 'fill the house with yodelling buffoons in leather shorts'. It is not kind, Humphrey!

But I must speak to you also about myself. Perhaps I cannot live much longer in the Nest. Miss Longridge is spending all day in the bedroom with her Inspector Reggie: my goodness, how they love each other! If only we were like them! They are like two turtle doves, billing and cooing. And all night I can hear our small Klaus crying to me out of the darkness, begging to be born.

Today on the Golf Course I was making a walk when Topp!…a golf ball has hit me on the head. Do not worry, dearest Humphrey, it is only a little lump. The man who has hit the ball has picked me up and felt my head. Should I have told him that I am engaged? He is rather like Kurt Jurgens, with a wicked moustache and a big smile. He has asked me to come to his castle with him and have dinner. Perhaps I shall go.

I wait for your letter. At the moment still
            your own

            Ursula.

P.S. Your Mama thanks you for your letter. She is in Albuhera Drive again with Frobisher the dog and tells me she has premonitions of great happiness.

Part Three

I have been walking all day. The Chaplain came to the gate to give me five shillings and an autographed copy of the *Posse from Galilee*, fresh and sweet-scented in a clean paper dust-jacket, and stood waving as I walked away.

Looking back from the top of the hill at the prison, a child's toy among Lilliput meadows, I felt a pang of separation. Then I turned away with the wind in my face and looked up at the great tumbled sky, nimbus and cumulo-nimbus, hammerheads of thunderclouds, dove-greys and silver-edged violet, threatening rain. And below the folded hills and dells and deserted fields, running away along the limestone watershed to Borchester and the sea. And between these great presences the darting, invisible song of the lark, lifted and lulled on the wind with the huge drifting shadows of the clouds

My Veldschoen were already white with chalkdust when I left the tarmacadam and took the old rough track across the hump-backed hills to Mundham, by way of Ambridge and the Roman Road. Torn turf trodden by Joseph of Arimathea, if we are to believe Huw of Gloucester in his bird-bright, rose-twining enamelled manuscript that lies in the Old Library at Stroud. Up in the hills where the wind tosses the gorse, the ancient ghost-wind of the Celts, sighing for the white bones of the early dead. And after half an hour I found myself at the top of a rise, looking down into a great flat bowl of England

England! I took from my battered suitcase a square of chocolate and munched it while my eyes traversed the horizon. The drowsy hum of the dumbledore was missing now in the early spring. The land was still brown, parched and sullen, and yet already patches of acid green proclaimed Spring's coming victory. A reverberating bang from a stone quarry behind the hills followed by a faint scream reminded me that I was not alone in the universe, but that at least there was now one less than a moment before. The echoes rolled away with the clouds, and the sunlight slipped up to me across the empty fields. The haze of green from the spring sowing, and high in the blue the lark. I shouldered my suitcase and swung off down the hill, the rhythm of my tramping feet bringing an old song to mind that rose in me irrepressibly, bursting from my lips like a shout:

> 'I love to go a-wandering
> My knapsack on my back...'

I have forgotten the rest, but I shouted the two lines over and over again, exulting. I was alone, between two prisons. Back at Droxford the girls would be banging their aluminium pans, and clattering the knives and forks out on the tables for lunch; at home Mrs Peacock would be picking mint in the back garden, and Miss Koch would be decorating my room. But now, here, I was inviolate.

At the bottom of the valley I could see a silver stream curving between crumbling banks. Thirst was gluey on my lips and I quickened my pace towards that cool purity. I was running now, over the dusty clods of a harrowed field. My suitcase banged against my legs. I tore at my collar, pulling off a button. I stumbled and ran on, reaching the edge of the field and rolling down a grassy bank, over and over, losing my suitcase, clutching at roots and laughing, rolling down towards the water and stopping, to my bruised and happy bewilderment, at the very brink of the stream. I bent and sucked the water through my lips, feeling it gurgle up my nostrils, then into my ears. Lifting my head, the water trickling off my chin and down my neck, I saw the dancing elements of my reflection recompose themselves and a pale face gazed at me against a patch of blue sky.

I watched my reflection floating on the evenly flowing surface of the stream, and felt a moment of such urgent and yet serene self-recognition that it was as if time itself were for a second suspended. History was now. Here was Humphrey Mackevoy, mirrored for a moment in water that was never still, that could never sustain the same image for a millionth of an instant, and yet the face remained, it was real and had meaning. I saw myself against flux and was preserved. As I bent closer to look more deeply into my own eyes the crumbling earth of the bank gave way, and I found myself up to the elbows in cold water, gazing now at swirling mud. I laughed, and clumsily backed up the bank and threw myself down in the warm grass, drying my hands on tussocks.

I was not surprised to see that I was in the exact centre of a crucible of hills. I looked up at the rim where I had been an hour before, now scarcely higher from where I lay than the grass about my head. High above me the lark still rose and fell on the wind, but in my bed of grass I was sheltered. A ladybird an inch away, clinging to a stalk, half-opened its red wing-cases to reveal an edge of glinting gossamer and closed them again with a minuscule shrug.

I was suddenly cold as a cloud crossed the sun. Something at the back of my mind made me uneasy. It was not the far-off thought of Mundham, or any fear of the future. It was not even the knowledge of my own impermanence. Something was missing. I noticed that I was stroking with my forefinger a little palm of grass and realized what it was: there were no trees in the landscape. I sat up impatiently. My suitcase lay lopsided in the grass higher up the bank. Looking round the bowl of green hills and the fields that sloped down towards me I thought how little I had wanted a tree all day. There was not even a

175

sapling in sight but I had been happy. I knew that I loved everything, from each green stalk of grass to the highest redwood with the undemanding love of a brother. I lay down again and must have fallen asleep.

When I awoke the sun was colder. I picked up my suitcase and trudged towards it, westward into the hills, relishing the dark bitter taste of my last square of chocolate, up and over the rim. Ambridge was there, in the next valley, grey roofs and a steeple under the declining sun, and down below me the confident white barns of Brookfield Farm. I did not envy them their quiet security, for I was for the dark.

I saw my first tree of the day three miles further on. Coming down out of the hills I found a deserted church, roofless and with a broken tower, and beside it a yew tree. It had to be yew. How many summer mornings had found me in the old churchyard at Mundham, breathing in the closeness of the musky evergreen, half listening to the early birdsong as the sun stealthily established its golden disc in the grey dawn. Today I only ran my hand over the red bark and touched my cheek against it with the passionless decorum of one French admiral greeting another in the street. I ate my sausage sandwiches sitting on a gravestone, resting and thinking of death.

On into the golden evening. I bought a choc-ice from a van parked outside a lonely cottage and sucked it along the road to Borchester. There were plenty of trees here, grey poplar and willow, ash and evergreen oak, and I gave them all a friendly wave. The flavour of the choc-ice reminded me of afternoons with Dad in the sorting office, and his rueful chuckles at registered parcels so smeared with chocolate that he could not read the address. I determined to sleep out, and began to look for a likely spot. There were small houses along the road now, with gardens and orchards, and finally this place, a wood of conifers, carpeted with pine-needles stretching down from the road to a dark pond. I am sitting with my back against a Scots pine. How different it would have been in the old days! The peace is inexpressible. It is so dark now that I can hardly see to write. I feel calm, tired, and weirdly un-aroused by the presence of these brooding Gymnosperms. Perhaps I am saved.

Alas not. As I put my notebook back in my suitcase and settled my head on it to sleep I became aware that an insect had crawled up my trouser leg and was swinging like a gibbon through my pubic hair, bent on mischief. Taking off my trousers to investigate, I felt the cool night air waft resinous perfume around my tickling parts. It was enough to try a saint. Quickly and clinically I dispatched the ant – for ant it proved to be – and wriggled into my trousers as fast as I could. Fortunately the peace of the night and my extreme tiredness has now caused the erection to subside. But what of tomorrow?

EXCERPT FROM THE DIARY OF HUMPHREY MACKEVOY

I am writing this by the light of a fire of green logs, and the whine and splutter of the damp wood burning makes my hand unsteady. I am grateful for the warmth in the darkness, but at what a price! Sitting round the fire with me are four men in blue donkey jackets and caps, drinking strong tea and rolling cigarettes. I feel as great a distaste for each of them as I ever felt for Mr Smart: I can hardly bear their presence, they offend me so deeply, as does the smell of the woodsmoke and the scream of the logs. To be sitting, apparently calmly, in an encampment of woodcutters! But I must stay. I feel it is a vigil.

It is a relief to be able to record the events of the day, under the pretext that I am writing to a 'sweetheart', and so avoid the burden of making conversation. I woke up this morning so stiff in every sense that I could hardly move. At first I thought I was dreaming, and expected the branches, dark against the pale dawn sky, to fade away and be replaced by the waking certainty of the bare bulb in the ceiling of my cell. After a few seconds memory returned. My face was unpleasantly damp, and the dawn chorus blared in my ears in a cacophony of throaty warbling and shrill, repetitive trills.

My back was sore against the dusty bark of the pine tree, but scrambled messages of erotic suggestion were decoding themselves in my bruised mind. The messages, I realized, were being transmitted by my tethered mast which had erected itself to wake me. Still half conscious I reacted instinctively, half groping for the drill in the pine needles as I had done that morning in the Arboretum at Nottingham, where after a night of slippery delight I had slumped asleep at the foot of a bald cypress. Waking with the smell of the trees in my nostrils I had turned the drill dreamily without moving, choosing a cleft between two roots: it was the only time that I had ever made love lying down, but I had not the energy to stand.

This morning there was no drill among the needles, and by the time I realized this, the censor was awake. I shook myself to my feet and staggered between the regular trunks, fleeing like a small child from an enchanted forest. I didn't stop until I was some way along the road, and then only to loosen my shoelaces and urinate into a bottomless bucket in a ditch.

I had hardly eaten the day before, and I was glad to come across a corrugated iron building with 'Café' written on the roof. I sat down, fortunately alone for it was very early, to a plate of fried egg, bacon, beans and fried bread. For the first time since leaving prison I began to ask myself where I was going and what I was going to do when I got there. My little shop was gone, as was my social position at Mundham, much of my self-respect and the old irresponsibilities of my unbridled nature. The smell of the baked beans reminded me of Mother. How would I bear the confinement, condemned to trudge between Mummy's foetid room and the importunities of Miss Koch? A monster, a useless son, a pariah, a parasite.

I decided I must escape. To a place where I could start again, and at the same time avoid temptation. Some treeless place: Orkney perhaps, or the Sahara, Antarctica, Anapurna or the Great Outback. As my hunger retreated before the assaulting hordes of baked beans another, deeper hunger took its place. I looked through the grimy window of the café at a sturdy lime tree and felt my belly tremble. Beyond it a frail coppice of beeches, fragile green, and beyond them up along the smudge of hillside the dark saw-teeth of a fir windbreak. I was sore-eyed for lack of sleep, and while my testes whirred like twin dynamos my brain struggled to rouse its white-coated boffin and send him clattering down the spiral nerves to switch off the power at the mains. I knew, rationally, that I must spend the whole day, in whatever direction I travelled, wandering like a sailor, newly home from an immense voyage, among these sylvan brothels, and was terrified.

I gripped the plastic-topped table, and longed insanely to stay in that steam-gurgling corrugated cave. I tried to smother desire with helping after helping of flatulent carbohydrate. It was much later that I heard a familiar voice, switched on in mid-sentence by the butter-fingered sandwich-cutter at the counter, describing a new Australian invention for peeling potatoes. Its fruity confidence was unmistakable. It was Jack de Manio, sailing over the air-waves with his cargo of news, curios and popular wisdom. Memories leaped to mind like iron-filings to a magnet: Nat

JOHN FORTUNE & JOHN WELLS

and Bee, Mummy brawling on the lawn, Inspector Stoneley, that evening waiting for bluff Jack at Bars, and the cool, voluptuous mystery of my Tree of Heaven.

The memories beat on my mind, an intolerable tolling of regret and nostalgia, memories of the days when I was happy and there was no guilt, when each harsh twist of the drill, each savage thrust of the pelvis, each moist withdrawal was an affirmation of myself. Where was I now? Torn between guilt and guilt, between the guilty act and the grudgingly self-imposed abstinence. I began to wonder whether I had inherited Mummy's fears about her own identity. Jack de Manio's voice was torturing me. I stood indecisive, and then made to go. The proprietor called after me, asking me to leave the door ajar.

I walked like a drunkard, trying to concentrate on putting one foot in front of the other, muttering bits of old rhymes and nursery songs to occupy my mind. Out of the corners of my eyes I could see the shadows of trees, pale colonnades of trunks, boughs and roots and exciting glimpses of forking branch behind the crisp tracery of new green. Along lanes brushing the foliage with my finger-tips until the lane dwindled to a cart-track I ran the green gauntlet between springy sprays of blackthorn and young beech, smelling the scent of the rowan and the may after a shower of rain.

Then, under the sun, I watched my shadow shorten, stumbling on through the wet grass, across misty fields of young corn, ducking blindly through barriers of branches, desperate to find the main road. As I went I tried again to ask myself what I was going to do back in Mundham: but again and again, whenever I tried to form a rational plan, scenes of past debauch filled my mind with obscene projections, three-dimensional sounds and smells and old ejaculations. Desire, as I walked, weighed me down. I was becoming exhausted, and I could only dimly hope that the temptation itself would prove so tiring that I should not have the energy to give in to it.

I stopped, panting, in a woody dell where a rusted breakdown lorry with broken windows leaned in the stillness. Automatically I looked the nearest tree up and down. It was an elm, and was dying, having been struck by lightning and split down the length of its trunk. My mind leaped to think of the power that had fallen from above and scorched this giant, opening its veins to the sky. Divine plunder! Hissing from the topmost twigs, burning blue down, down through the tortured wood, raping this arbitrary victim in a clap of thunder.

In the moist silence I laid my tongue to the cleft. The exposed heartwood was dry and cold, the sap had left it. Still my tongue searched on, and my fingertips strayed obscenely, fluttering round bare knots, erring in cobwebs. A dead woodlouse was dislodged above me, and rattled down into silence. Excited by the tree's helplessness I began to undo my buttons. As my penis brushed the opening it was as though the electricity remained in it, and delicious shocks played over the backs of my thighs. I was grateful for my rubber-soled shoes. How could this be wrong? The tree was dying. I was merely paying it my last respects. Then, from far away, I heard the wailing of a circular saw, ringing as it cut into the wood. I shrank, and fumbled with my buttons like a guilty thing surprised. I felt sick, and rested my forehead against the bark. The Furies that had pursued me since the day of Labby's death flapped in the air above me and I retched.

I knew that a crisis was approaching. I blundered towards the far-off noise, seeing in my mind's eye the lopped and naked trunks, trembling and then falling before the banal insistence of the spinning steel. In my nausea, dark patches floated at the periphery of my vision. With a drunkard's luck I found the road. Huge lorries rushed past me. I seemed to be on the outskirts of a small town. There were neat gardens, with tulips and daffodils, and yes, there were laburnums too. I saw the beginnings of the yellow golden chains. My chains, invisible, on which I was being led back captive, to the dreaded reunion, the battlefield, the imperial past.

The noise of the saw, still so far away, whined in my ears above the noise of the passing lorries. There was a public garden, a war memorial and a notice board on a green post with Bye-Laws in indecipherable small print. A shop with toy aeroplanes hanging in the window, a butcher's, a newsagent's. Still the noise of the saw. I began to run, my suitcase bumping against my thigh. Past the empty car park of a shuttered pub, past the gateway of a school where children waiting for the bus stood and stared at me as I ran, past more gardens and more bungalows, until I came to a muddy track where the level of noise told me that I had found the sacrilege.

I rushed into a place that reminded me of old photographs of the Somme: branches with new leaves lay everywhere, torn from the trunks, a fire was burning, and there was a clearing full of fresh stumps. There were two men in the clearing, bent over a fallen tree, sawing it into lengths. The other two were stacking logs, and stopped as I ran up, turning to look at me in silence. I thought first, in a mad rage, that I would kill them: then one of them came towards me, and I began to tremble uncontrollably. I asked him what the time was and he said it was knocking-off time.

They talked to me as if I was a half-wit, offering me a cup of tea and asking me where I was making for. They told me that Mundham was twenty miles away, the other side of Reading. I must have seemed in great distress, for without any further questions they clapped me on the back and asked me to sit by their fire. I think they were Irish. I half listened to their talk for a very long time, and then suddenly asked them how they could be so cruel to the trees. Their leader, a red-faced man with blue eyes, laughed and tipped the dregs of his tea hissing into the fire. He said that the trees themselves were cruel, fighting for the sunlight and the air and exterminating every sapling too weak to oppose them.

I could find no answer to his argument. It was after all necessary to him to kill trees. I tried to understand, to feel sympathy with them as I sat in their company, but looking beyond the circle of firelight I felt only a kinship with the ancient heritage of the forest, and despair at the futility of man.

They have stopped talking now, and have rolled themselves in their blankets. I am left looking at the ash whitening at the edge of the small fire.

It is now five-thirty in the morning. I am writing this in the Waiting Room of the Bus Station in Reading. The first bus to Mundham goes at six-fifteen. It is very cold, and my companions in the Waiting Room are all down and outs in torn overcoats, sleeping on the benches or with their head in their arms on the table. Such is the state of my member that I am almost unable to shift my position, and standing up or sitting down is agony. It is bruised, and deliciously lacerated.

It seems so long ago now that I was sitting in that alien clearing embarrassed by the uninhibited exhalations of the woodmen preparing for sleep. Several hours of inactivity in that warm, perjured glow had rested my body, and my numbed mind was gradually nudged into active reverie by my restored forces. The wood-smoke that until then had reeked of death and the funeral pyre drifted across me as the red glow faded in the darkness, and brought with it hints of perfume, musk and invitation. I remember tiptoeing from the fire.

The man who stopped to offer me a lift on the main road was apparently as mad as I was. He told me as he accelerated grimly round blind corners of the winding road that his wife was about to have a baby in Reading General Hospital. He was clearly distraught, so much so that it was only after several tyre-screaming miles that he realized she was not in the back of the car. He put me down for no reason that I could understand by a scrap metal yard in the outskirts of the town, and after reversing in a series of desperate shunts, roared off in the direction from which we had come.

I was desperate, and had not felt such animal excitement since that horrid night by the reservoir. I looked in both directions. There was not a tree in sight. In an incoherent panic I realized that I had no drill with me. I rummaged among the scrap metal, and found at last a rusted iron railing, from which I was able to detach a single bar with an arrowhead spike. I began to run.

After street upon street of barren concrete, pavement, gutter and asphalt I found in a strip of front garden a young cherry tree, *prunus avium*. I had to be furtive, as through the lace curtains I could see a couple moving on a low sofa in the glow of the television. I touched the bark with my iron spear, and was about to hurl my weight behind it, gouging and scraping, when I stopped, dropped the iron railing, and knelt.

Transfigured before me was Labby in glory.

I had vowed that I would never touch another tree. Remorsefully I backed away, and as I did so the yellow golden chains began to fade and I saw again a sooty cherry tree in the darkness.

I felt that I was doomed.

I wandered, desolate, my quivering manhood leading me like a diviner's wand through that desert of cement. At last, unhinged I think, I saw the gaping mouth of a pillar box, and vaulted on to it. Lying on its flat top, I fumbled with my buttons and pushed my member through the letter box. Pox on it! I found to my humiliation that the aperture was too large. I slid to the ground, and kicked it till my foot was sore. Then I limped off down the road in search of anything that might give me peace.

It was beginning to rain. I tried the letter box of a private house with a diabolic spring: a milk bottle I found on a step, and at last, after inspecting dozens, a swan-necked lamp-post with a hole roughly the right size but a good twelve inches too low. I roarod my delight at finding it, and crouching in the harsh sodium light, rammed home into that unyielding concrete, ten times more terrible than teak. It was like being thrown naked through a plateglass window, but I went in and out and in and out.

An occasional car swished past, throwing up a plume of muddy water that soaked me. I was beginning to hate Reading and this horrible lamp-post. If it were not, for me, that the process leading to ejaculation once started cannot be stopped, I would have withdrawn there and then and slunk away. As it was I winced and grimaced, crouching at that concrete trunk, and once mistakenly trying to bite it. Then, as an articulated lorry drenched me from head to foot three times in rhythmic succession, I felt the orgasm gathering in me, tiny trickles from far-off nerves that formed rivulets, then rivers, and crashed through the flood-gates in a tidal bore of relief.

My clothes are still soaking and filthy, and the pain is considerable, but it is as nothing compared with the agonies of frustration that I experienced earlier. One thing that is a source of great pride to me is that I have been true to my Labby. I have kept my word.

EXCERPT FROM THE DIARY OF HUMPHREY MACKEVOY

I had to touch him before I could believe it. Dad is back.

I caught the early bus from Reading, and got here just after seven. The curtains were still drawn in the front room, and there was a smell about the house that somehow recalled my earliest childhood. I riddled the Aga, and began to make breakfast for Mummy and me. I heard a tread on the stairs that should have startled me, but it was so familiar from thirty years ago that I was not even surprised when the door opened and Dad came in in his dressing-gown, smoking his pipe. Then it was like seeing an old film again that one had forgotten and yet remembered in every detail. Nothing had changed. There was not a grey hair in his moustache, and his hair was still parted as I had seen it in the photographs.

He shook my hand and told me that I had grown. Then I heard Mummy coming downstairs singing as she used to in the old days, and she came and kissed me. Her eye was healed, and as she held my father's hand and kissed him I thought she looked years younger. Then over breakfast they told me how Dad had found himself after the avalanche in an enclosed valley in the mountains, being looked after by blue-robed monks in a monastery by a lake. The climate was wonderful, and it seemed to suit his health. He spent the days walking in the mountains, watching the giant pandas ambling through the bamboo groves. He had learned the language of the monks, and helped them to catalogue their library.

He had asked again and again if he could communicate with Mummy, and had at last been given permission to come and fetch her to go and live with him. They are leaving tomorrow for Liverpool. Dad was not in the least put out by what I had done, but advised me that if I wanted to continue I should go and live in some secluded place. Perhaps if all went well the monks might be persuaded to have me to live with them in the valley one day. They are both upstairs now, packing.

This morning a man came to see me who tells me he is engaged to be married to Miss Koch. He is short and bald and rather nice, and he is the new professional at the Golf Course. He said that Miss Koch's parents have been to see our house and wanted to buy it. They have offered five thousand pounds and Dad has advised me to accept it. The Insurance Company has agreed to settle Mummy's claim for the shop and its contents for twelve thousand.

Dad and Mum and I had lunch in the dining room and talked about old times, and afterwards I went out for a walk on my own, trying not to look at Labby's stump as I passed it. Several people recognized me and smiled in greeting, and in the park I saw Rose Hopkins with her husband and a sailor I took to be her brother. She is expecting a baby.

I called at the Nest on the way home to congratulate Miss Koch on her engagement. She was not there, but I had tea with Ethne, who was looking tired but wonderfully content. She said I had been very naughty and deserved 'a good spanking' but smilingly forgave me. Later she talked of a double wedding. She told me that Doris Strangeways is also to be married to Bob Makins, and that Pia Smart has become a Protestant and is now housekeeper to Archdeacon Horns, who has moved to Woolwich. Sitting and drinking tea with the old lady I felt a great affection for her, and remembered that wild afternoon with the vodka and the zither music. She laughed at the memory of it.

I saw Mrs Peacock working in the garden when I got back, and she was unusually friendly. She told me that by a strange coincidence Mr Peacock is at Droxford for embezzlement, and wanted to know all about the food and the warders.

This evening, just before supper, I did go out to see Labby. The sun was going down behind the gardens, and all the fences were edged with gold. I knelt down in front of the stump, and was about to touch it with my lips when I saw the tiny beginnings of a bud. My eyes brimmed, and I gazed at it with wonder, and as the sinking sun gilded the tiny pink clouds in the wide blue evening sky, it was as if a voice was whispering: 'Be of good comfort, for I am in all trees; love me in them!'

Afterword

It was two months before I found this cottage, deep in a dell of deciduous darlings, lapped in their russet drifts in autumn and surrounded in spring by a carpet of primroses. It is small and well-roofed, simple and orderly. I have a few books, and a little table by the window here where I write from time to time.

As I look through the letters and yellowing newspaper cuttings and the pieces of paper covered with writing in various hands that I have selected for their bearing on my story, I notice with a fastidious shudder an excremental theme that patterns the narrative like an inlay of umber chalcedony. But meditating on this I find it only fitting that such a theme should be present, and even prominent, in any description of my fellow men.

Not so with trees. As I gaze on them now through the open window, with the spring air teasing the leaves from their buds and the whole wood echoing with birdsong, I am rapt as I have been all my life at their clean beauty and infinite variety. I recognize the mystical presence of Labby in every tree in the forest, and something the Irish woodcutter said has made my lovemaking even more urgent and unrepentant since I made that discovery. He was right to say that trees are selfish and cruel in their magnificent celebration of their own nature, and as I drive home the drill I know that I am guiltless in celebrating mine.

So stand, my sylvan beauties! In the insect hum of

189

summer I have had you, wet with sweat in the long afternoons, wrestling with the endless tossing of your branches, cooled by the tree-made breeze, breathing deep the smell of green perfection as the whole forest sways to a slow pavan: far into the scented nights, the dappled moonlight glinting on my drill as I lifted the elm with my pelvis. I have had you in the autumn, when the thwock thwock thwock of my member sounded in the still frosty air. And in the winter, in the short days, when the black branches are covered with snow against the rook-cawing grey sky, I have dislodged it by boughfuls as I stood naked and thigh-deep in a cold drift, my scrotum chilled with each withdrawal. And now in the spring, the sap rises. Although I am no longer young I bite the growing bark in ecstasy, and mould my flesh to it, crying for my laburnum as my own sap rises, and I am renewed.

PRION HUMOUR CLASSICS

AUGUSTUS CARP ESQ
Henry Howarth Bashford
introduced by Robert Robinson
"much funnier and darker than *Diary of a Nobody*, with which it is
often compared" *Independent on Sunday*
1-85375-411-0

SEVEN MEN AND TWO OTHERS
Max Beerbohm
introduced by Nigel Williams
"the funniest book about literature ever written" Nigel Williams
1-85375-415-3

HOW TO TRAVEL INCOGNITO
Ludwig Bemelmans
introduced by Robert Wernick
"a complete original" *Saturday Review*
1-85375-419-6

MAPP AND LUCIA
E F Benson
introduced by Stephen Pile
"a wonderously bitchy caricature of upper class
English manners" *The Scotsman*
1-85375-390-4

THE FREAKS OF MAYFAIR
E F Benson
introduced by Brian Masters
"acid-tongued… peerless" *Kirkus Review*
1-85375-429-3

THE MARSH MARLOWE LETTERS
Craig Brown
introduced by Craig Brown
"I doubt there is a better parodist alive" Matthew Paris, *The Spectator*
1-85375-461-7

HOW STEEPLE SINDERBY WANDERERS WON THE FA CUP
J L Carr
introduced by D J Taylor
"a wonderful book" *The Observer*
1-85375-363-7

DIARY OF A PROVINCIAL LADY *
E M Delafield
introduced by Jilly Cooper
"an incredibly funny social satire… the natural predecessor to
Bridget Jones" *The Times*
1-85375-368-8

THE PAPERS OF A J WENTWORTH, BA
H F Ellis
introduced by Miles Kington
"a gloriously funny account of the day-to-day life
of an earnest, humourless and largely ineffective
school master" *The Daily Mail*
1-85375-398-X

SQUIRE HAGGARD'S JOURNAL
Michael Green
introduced by the author
"marvellously funny spoof of the 18th-century
diarists" *The Times*
1-85375-399-8

THE DIARY OF A NOBODY
George and Weedon Grossmith
introduced by William Trevor
"a kind of Victorian Victor Meldrew" *The Guardian*
1-85375-364-5

THREE MEN IN A BOAT
Jerome K Jerome
introduced by Nigel Williams
"the only book I've fallen off a chair laughing at"
Vic Reeves
1-85375-371-8

MRS CAUDLE'S CURTAIN LECTURES
Douglas Jerrold
introduced by Peter Ackroyd
"one of the funniest books in the language"
 Anthony Burgess
1-85375-400-5

THE UNSPEAKABLE SKIPTON
Pamela Hansford Johnson
introduced by Ruth Rendell
"A superb comic creation."
The New Statesman
1-85375-471-4

SUNSHINE SKETCHES OF A LITTLE TOWN
Stephen Leacock
introduced by Mordecai Richler
"there is no-one quite like Leacock, and no-one quite so good"
Tatler
1-85375-367-X

NO MOTHER TO GUIDE HER
Anita Loos
introduced by Kathy Lette
"classic and even funnier than Loos's *Gentlemen Prefer Blondes*"
The Independent
1-85375-366-1

HERE'S LUCK
Lennie Lower
"Australia's funniest book" Cyril Pearl
1-85375-428-5

THE AUTOBIOGRAPHY OF A CAD
A G Macdonell
introduced by Simon Hoggart
"wonderfully sharp, clever, funny and cutting"
Simon Hoggart
1-85375-414-5

THE SERIAL *
Cyra McFadden
introduced by the author
"an American comic masterpiece" *The Spectator*
1-85375-383-1

THE WORLD OF S J PERELMAN *
S J Perelman
introduced by Woody Allen
"the funniest writer in America" Gore Vidal
1-85375-384-X

THE EDUCATION OF HYMAN KAPLAN *
Leo Rosten
introduced by Howard Jacobson
"the funniest, sweetest and most ingenious book ever written"
Mail on Sunday
1-85375-382-3

THE RETURN OF HYMAN KAPLAN *
Leo Rosten
introduced by Howard Jacobson
"exquisitely funny" Evelyn Waugh
1-85375-391-2

THE UNREST-CURE AND OTHER BEASTLY TALES
Saki
introduced by Will Self
"they dazzle and delight" Graham Greene
1-85375-370-X

THE ENGLISH GENTLEMAN
Douglas Sutherland
"extremely funny" Jilly Cooper
1-85375-418-8

* for copyright reasons these titles are not available in the USA or
Canada in the Prion edition.